MEET YOUR MATCH

MATCHING MILLIONS
BOOK ONE

BROOKLYN BELL

Published 2023 by Copper House Press

www.copperhousepress.com

ISBN: 979-8-9878455-2-3

Any references to historical events, real people, or real places are used fictitiously. Names, characters, and places are products of the author's imagination.

Cover design by Damonza

First printing, June 2023

1

"Are you sure Elle isn't asking for the full … what's it called again?"

Danny pulls his lips away from mine just long enough to get the question out. Then he's covering my mouth with his again, kissing me harder as he pushes me up against the wall of the dark hallway.

We're deep inside the bow of the ship—so deep that I can't even feel the water rocking beneath the yacht anymore.

Now it's my turn to pull away from him to answer.

"You mean a Full 360 Audition?" I lean back breathlessly, just far enough to look up at him. His dark brown eyes play with mine like he's toying with the idea of going all the way. Right here, right now, in the ship's hallway.

"Yeah, whatever it is that you called it back in the States at that first dinner we went to," he says before pulling me back in again, kissing me so urgently, so deliciously, that I nearly forget what type of matchmaking service my client, Elle, requested me to complete with him.

He grabs the back of my thighs and hoists me up so that my legs are wrapped around his waist while my back presses hard against the interior ship wall. Someone could walk by at any moment.

Guests have been making their way onboard the ship all day. Tonight's party is already getting underway, but I can't resist when a man takes the reins with me like this. This type of hook-up style is the number-one request I get from the women I help find partners for as a professional matchmaker. They want a man who will savagely seduce them—and then dominate them. And Elle is going to love getting tossed around like this by Danny once I officially hand him over to her.

Danny sets me back down and spins me around so fast, my face is nearly pressed against the wall as he leans into me from behind. I brace my hands against the cold fiberglass while he starts kissing the nape of my neck. Shockwaves flood my body with every nip and kiss. I have to push harder against the wall to keep my knees from buckling beneath me.

Elle specifically requested that Danny's matchmaking audition not reach the Full 360 mark. Which means we need to stop short of sex, or anything that might be considered sex. So if I let this go any farther, it's going to be too hard to stop that ball from rolling forward. Not just for him, but for both of us.

He slowly slides my dress strap across my shoulder. I close my eyes and zero in on his fingertips trailing along my collarbone. The strap loosens as it slides off—dropping lightly against my shoulder.

"Danny?" I draw out his name like a school teacher at the start of a soft scolding. He instantly pauses—his lips hovering above my bare shoulder. Then he pushes my dress strap back up into place. "Good boy," I say, smiling.

"We really can't—?" he says, dragging another slow kiss across my skin.

"You've officially passed your audition," I say triumphantly, turning around to face him. My body aches for him to keep touching me, but I can't let him. Instead, I grin and gently pull his hands away from where they're still pressed against my hips.

A regretful smile stretches across his impossibly handsome features. He reminds me of the actor Regé-Jean Page.

"All this is for you to be matched with Elle." I remind him gently. "You've already passed. And Elle doesn't want the Full 360. There's no reason for you and me to go any farther right now."

"I can think of at least one reason," he says, looking down at the bulge that's appeared between us, then back up at me with a sideways grin. We both laugh as I duck out from under one of his arms.

Danny looks up at the ceiling with a sigh as another laugh escapes his dark, pillowy lips. "Cher Thatcher. World's most infamous tease," he says good-naturedly then shakes his head in disbelief.

"The one and only. At your service." I grin back at him.

He drapes his arm lightly around my waist and I lean into him as we make our way down the long hall, back to the party getting underway on deck.

"It'll be worth it in the long run," I say, smiling at him. He's not the first man I've had to let down easy right in the middle of a hot makeout session. This one was hot enough for both of us to think twice about stopping. He's an incredible kisser. And those hands of his … If I'd let him continue, I guarantee he wouldn't have disappointed me in the least. "Elle really is your perfect match. I promise. I'll have my assistant Daisy get the two of you set up on your first official date soon."

The music at the end of the hallway starts thumping as the light under the doorway grows brighter. It sounds like Rory Grant is kicking off the first night aboard Owen's yacht on the party deck. I loved her last Grammy award-winning single and I hope we're getting back out to the party before she's too far into her set of greatest hits.

"When do you head back to Malibu?" I ask Danny.

"I only flew out here for tonight," he says, giving my waist a squeeze. He's being a good sport about stopping short like a couple of teenagers getting caught right before their curfew. The feeling I had about him must have been right if he's handling this with such grace. Daisy was actually the one to suggest him for one of my newer VIP clients, actress Elle Franetti, and she was right. His easy-going nature is going to complement Elle well.

When we get to the end of the hall, Danny opens the door for us, and light floods into the dark hallway. We both pause to take in the scene unfolding before us outside the open door.

"Wow," he mutters breathlessly. I grin at him as his jaw hangs open slightly. "Owen really … I mean, wow." I wait for him to come up with the perfect word to describe Owen's party, but he trails off without finishing the thought.

"Yes, he really does," I say, knowing what he means since I can't find the right words to describe it, either.

The party deck of Owen's seven-hundred-foot megayacht has been transformed.

Thousands of tiny white lights are strung across every foot of airspace, while thousands more have been wrapped around a half-dozen gorgeous—and fully grown—Bonaventure umbrella trees Owen had flown in from the nearby shores of Saint-Tropez. There's a tall stage set up on one side of the deck with Rory Grant belting out one of her biggest party hits of all time while at least a hundred guests are jumping up and down across the dance floor to the beat of her music.

Uniformed crew members are passing out trays of crystal champagne flutes to any guests sitting still long enough to grab one. And at least five fully staffed bar tops are overflowing with top-shelf alcohol, complete with a long line of Dom Perignon and Crystal bottles set across the back waiting to be poured.

The infinity pool to our left is backlit with black lights and has foamy bubbles spilling out over the sides. Danny and I watch as a topless model I recognize as the runner-up from a popular reality TV show lets out a whoop and dives head-first down the two-story water slide into the deep end. The crowd near the pool cheers that's loud enough to be heard over the enormous but expertly hidden speakers surrounding us.

Danny finally looks back at me with wide eyes. "Owen really goes all out."

I grin happily. "That's my Owen."

This is going to be a wickedly fun week.

As if on cue, Owen emerges from the dance floor. His eyes find me immediately.

He could easily pass for a Venroy model in a cream linen Dior suit tailored just above his ankles, and soft leather boat shoes. I notice that his signature dirty-blonde shag has grown just a bit shaggier for this trip, but it suits him well. Too well. His smooth skin is already kissed by the Saint-Tropez sun—setting off his impossibly light blue eyes.

If I didn't know Owen like I do, I'd guess he was just a surfer boy off the Santa Monica pier all dressed up for a night out on the town.

But I do know him. And he's no surfer boy. He's the owner of this itty bitty floating city we're on, and my very best friend in the world.

I saunter over to him, my canary-yellow Prada gown flowing in the breeze, and stretch up onto my nude Louboutins, managing to kiss him gently on the cheek.

"There you are, babe," I say with a grin. "Happy Birthday!"

2

"It's the woman of the hour," Owen says, kissing me back on the cheek.

"Oh whatever." I push him away playfully. "It's your birthday. Not mine."

"The fact that I got you out here on the *MaryLou* this week is my gift," he says with a grin, grabbing my face tenderly between his hands.

Owen designed this ship himself and then named it after his adoring mother, Mary, and the sweet nickname his father has called her for the past forty years. *MaryLou.* I've turned down the opportunity to join him out here countless times since he christened the ship two years ago, but this whole week was my idea—to host his birthday party on the ship in Saint-Tropez. It's Owen's favorite place in the world.

His clear blue eyes lock with mine as he pulls me closer to him. For a split second, I think he's going to kiss me. My stomach knots itself into a pretzel at the thought of it. But at the last moment, he stands up straighter and draws me into a big bear hug instead.

"Hey man, this party is unreal," Danny pipes up next to me.

"Glad you could make it," Owen says, clapping a hand on his shoulder. "Even if just for one night." Owen looks like a kid in a candy shop, and it reminds me of the sweet college kid he was when we first met: fourteen years ago, before we were even legally able to drink. Since then, he's become an internationally-desired billionaire that the tabloids can't get enough of.

He's called in a few favors to keep this party out of the gossip sites and magazines this week, and so far, I haven't seen a single paparazzi helicopter circling the ship. I'm guessing that's how he got so many of his powerful friends and business cohorts to join us out here, with the promise of a guilt-free, private week of fun and pleasure aboard Owen's luxury liner. In fact, hardly anyone from the guest list turned him down.

"Whoa, look out—" Owen pulls me against him just as four rowdy NBA players appear and start grabbing Danny, pushing him playfully toward the pool. Danny owns the Lakers, and I think I recognize a few of the guys from his team in the group.

"I'll watch out for Daisy's call," Danny calls back to me over his shoulder, laughing before letting himself be dragged away. I watch as they pretend to toss him into the pool, then hand him a shot glass of something clear. They all throw one back together, followed by a cheer.

I turn back to Owen who's watching me instead of the spectacle over by the pool.

"You look stunning tonight," he says softly.

"You don't look so bad yourself," I say, raising my brows back at him.

"How have you been feeling since you got out here?"

For a few moments, I'd forgotten that we were in the middle of the Mediterranean Sea.

"Pretty good," I say, taking a deep breath and putting on my best everything-is-fine smile. I don't want him to worry about me. He knows it's been ten years since the last time I set foot on a boat—and why. But that was a long time ago.

He pulls me toward him again to dodge a train of beautiful women parading past us holding hands. The girls make a tidal wave-sized splash as they all scream and jump into the foamy pool together. We both take a step back to avoid getting wet.

"I was afraid you might ditch out at the last minute."

"Nah. This was my idea," I remind him. Ideally, we'd all be loaded into some abandoned castle or ancient chapel ruins or some other glamorous location instead of partying out here on the water. But it's too late to change that now.

Regardless, I wouldn't have missed this for the world. Not only is this Owen's week-long birthday bash and biggest party of the year, but it's also going to be a phenomenal opportunity to nail down a few matches for my current VIP clients. With Elle officially matched to Danny, I have two women left on my current client list: Audra Franklin and Zara Cordon. Both have requested the Full 360 Audition for my matchmaking services, which just so happens to be the niche service that has made me famous—and a bit infamous—among this powerful crowd.

"Incoming," Owen says quietly while eyeing someone coming up behind me. "You're about to get girl-crush rushed in three ... two ..."

"Cher!" A woman squeals out my name. Without even turning around, I can already tell that the owner of the voice is a bit tipsy. Owen winks at me, holding back the slightest grin. I try to stifle my own grin before Mimi comes into view.

"Mimi!" I squeal back just as Mimi Darwin—formerly Mimi Creighton—circles me. "And Theo!" Mimi's new husband trails behind.

Owen steps back to give the three of us more room, but his eyes are still sparkling at me. He's clearly enjoying this little performance. Whenever a former client rushes over to gush about the man I matched her with, he calls it a *girl-crush rush*. And this one is well underway.

"Have I shown you this rock?" Mimi flips her hand up to my face so fast, she nearly hits me on the nose.

"A few times, but I never get tired of seeing it." I laugh and peek at Owen, who's stifling a laugh of his own, but his eyes are full of admiration.

"This man. This man you found me! Theo is just the *best*!" She wobbles on her feet.

Okay, so Mimi is more than a little tipsy. But she's happy. And I love seeing her ecstatic over the match I made for her with Theo.

"I'm so glad for you," I say, beaming genuinely at them. This is truly the best part of my job. Well, this, and getting to audition the most gorgeous, powerful men in the world. But moments like this are why I really love what I do.

"And I don't even have to tell you about what he's packing underneath that pair of chinos—" She side-eyes Theo's inseam with a whistle.

"Okay, okay, Mimi," Theo interjects, turning slightly red and rolling his eyes at me. He apologizes to us, then gives Mimi a kiss. Most likely to stop her from saying more for a moment, but in a sweet, embarrassed husband kind of way.

"You gave me true love, Cher." Mimi's slurring her words a little now, leaning in like we're old friends. "True. Love. I never would have found him all the way over in Croatia if you hadn't set us up."

Theo laughs. "Honey, I was born in Croatia, but I lived in New York when you met me," he reminds her.

"But, baby, your heart always stayed in Croatia. How would I have ever found it there?"

Owen walks around the group to stand next to me again. We watch Mimi and Theo together like two proud parents watching their children playfully bicker back and forth for a minute. Their chemistry is on point and I enjoy watching how they work out in real life—just like I knew it would in my head before I set them up.

"Is it ever weird to see the guy you matched after you two …" Owen whispers at me while Mimi and Theo continue swapping tipsy confessions of their love to each other.

I consider his question for a moment while eyeing Mimi's husband. Theo was what I like to call a *sleeping giant* in my profession. Sweet, quiet, and confident on the outside, but an absolute tiger in the bedroom. His type is very popular with my clients.

"Not really," I say. "It's just business." I excel at turning off any personal feelings I might feel toward a potential match. In fact, I haven't been in a personally romantic relationship since the last time I stepped foot on a boat. No coincidence there.

"Nothing like the business deals I get myself into." Owen chuckles.

Staring at the sweet couple before me, I break into a grin. "I really do love my job."

As the owner of Match 360, I run what many people consider the most elite matchmaking service in the world. And the Full 360 Audition package has become the most popular method of matching all my VIP clientele. It's something of a signature offering for my boutique matchmaking business.

My clients are all similar to Mimi: incredibly successful, single women. They come to me after exhausting themselves in the modern dating world. Either they're tired of trying to chase down top-notch men who turn out to be playboys, or they finally think they've found The One, only to have The One be as thrilling as a dead fish when he finally takes them to bed.

That's where I come in. It's my job to weed out the bad matches and give these women what they want. Complete satisfaction guaranteed. Bedroom auditions included.

I make my matches based on five matchmaking principles: Personality, Looks, Affluence, Relationship Potential, and Sex.

That last principle is what makes my service stand out from the rest. My matches are promised to be good in bed, and I make sure of that by giving most of my clients' matches a Full 360 Audition when requested.

My company started as a typical high-end matchmaking service—matching affluent women to their soulmates. But it morphed to include the Full 360 Audition after one of my most high-maintenance clients insisted that I test drive the, for lack of a better word, *merchandise,* before she'd be willing to be matched with anyone. I increased her package rate to an astronomical sum and took her perfect match to bed with me. The guy I was matching her with had zero qualms about proving his worth to me in the bedroom before I handed him over to her with the intimate knowledge that my client wouldn't be disappointed.

After the best sex of her life, followed by a multimillion-dollar wedding on his private island off the coast of Saint Thomas, she had told all her girlfriends about what I had done for her.

And thus my niche practice was born.

Now, I operate largely on reputation alone and only work with two or three VIP clients at a time while the rest of my clients sit on my ever-growing waitlist. Once I successfully match a current VIP, my assistant pulls another VIP off the waitlist. Then I focus my attention on finding their dream man. The process runs like clockwork with the help of my angel assistant Daisy back home in Malibu. Most matches are made within a few weeks. Especially since my detailed database of single men has grown considerably over the years.

Just as I'm about to excuse myself from Mimi and Theo, my phone buzzes against my thigh. Whoever decided to start putting pockets in cocktail dresses was a genius.

I glance down at my phone just as Audra Franklin's name pops up on the screen.

3

"Audra!" I say brightly as I answer the call. I hope she can hear me over the music.

I hold one finger up to Owen and mouth the words, *sorry, client*. Then I hurry across the deck to get as far away from the speakers as possible.

"You sound like you're at a party!"

I can barely hear her through the phone.

"It's Owen's birthday out on the yacht," I remind her. "It's night one. Rory Grant is here singing."

For the last three months, I've been trying to secure a match for Audra, who's proving to be my most challenging client of all time. In fact, this week I'm hoping to cross paths with someone I haven't presented to her yet while I'm on the *MaryLou*. I know Owen has invited more than a few promising bachelors.

"Oh, that's right," she says. "Wish I hadn't had to turn that invitation down, but this new product line is devouring all my time."

Audra is the owner of the biggest shapewear company in the world. I really like her, but she didn't exactly get to that level of success with an overly soft personality. Not only does she want a hot young billionaire-level businessman, but her match must also be willing to share her with other men during the occasional ménage à trois. A tall order, to say the least. And I've already exhausted my database of single executives and oil tycoons trying to find this needle in the haystack for her.

"I'm hoping to meet some new prospects on the ship. Someone I haven't thought of for you yet," I nearly shout into the phone.

"You're just going to have to call me later," she says. "I can hardly hear you. But yeah, I'd love a positive update sooner rather than later!"

As I click my phone off, the music comes to an end and I hear a microphone screech to life. Everyone around me groans and covers their ears.

"Hey everyone, I thought I'd start the week off by saying thank you to all of you for making it out here."

Owen has Rory's microphone on stage. His crystal clear eyes look almost translucent as he peers out at the crowd from within the spotlight. Rory is standing nearby grinning at him and someone from the crowd shouts out, "Owen! We love you!" while a few people start whooping.

"I love you too," he says deeply into the microphone. One of the girls from the crowd cheers, which sets off another wide grin from Owen.

"I just wanted to say a few words to get this party started," he says. "Huge thanks to the crew and the captain. They're all here to give us a good time this week and I, for one, am so grateful for all their hard work."

He goes on, thanking a few other people onboard, including his team who planned this whole week-long soiree. I tear my eyes away from him to survey the crowd of people around me. Everyone has a smile plastered to their face as they listen to him list everyone who's played a part in setting up this incredibly festive week to celebrate his birthday.

"And last but certainly not least, I'd like to thank my very best friend in the world, the stunning Cher Thatcher."

A few people glance in my direction. A woman pats my back from behind, and I feel myself start to blush.

"Cher, this whole thirty-fourth birthday party out here in this gorgeous place was all your idea. I know open water isn't your favorite thing." He pauses to smile warmly at me. "So I never would have agreed to all this if you weren't the one to suggest it. As a man who could have anything in the world— having you here to celebrate another year with me is all I really wanted."

A collective "Aww" spreads through the crowd, which makes me chuckle.

"To you, Cher." Owen holds up his glass. "And to all of you for making it out here."

A guy in the crowd yells, "Happy Birthday, Owen!"

"Happy Birthday!" the crowd echoes as they raise their glasses.

I lift my glass to take a sip with everyone else. Owen was right—I've been a little apprehensive about this week out on the water. But I couldn't be any happier than I am right now.

4

Rory's music set springs to life as Owen makes his way back toward me, greeting me with another hug and kiss—this time on top of my head.

"You didn't have to do that," I say.

"Do what?"

"Thank me in front of everyone like that."

"Oh, that wasn't my formal thank you yet," he says. "I have an actual gift for you, too." He's grinning at me sideways now. I can tell he's had a few drinks because he's getting a bit more playful and friskier than usual.

"You didn't need to get me a gift—" I start to say, but he interrupts me.

"I invited Channing Stanbury onboard this week."

"Channing Stanbury?" I yelp, then look around us quickly to make sure Channing himself isn't standing anywhere near us on deck wondering who just screamed out his name.

Owen starts laughing and swallows the rest of the champagne from his glass in one gulp.

"I couldn't just throw myself a party without giving you a gift, too." He laughs, staring out at the setting sun.

"I've been trying to nail down Channing for weeks!" I exclaim. "I think he could be a fantastic match for Audra."

Channing is an old-money, east coast billionaire with a reputation for being a little nontraditional in the bedroom. He's relatively new to the party scene in LA since he started taking on real estate projects out west, so it's been difficult for me to track him down.

"How? How did you get him to come here?" I ask, practically jumping up and down in excitement. This is exactly what I needed to hear to help me figure out Audra's match this week. I've been sensing her growing frustration as time passes on without a successful match lined up. If Channing Stanbury is on his way here, this could be a total game changer.

"He sold me that high rise on Park I told you about last week," Owen says. "We ended up having a drink after the deal went through. Turns out, he just purchased that huge new project on Coastline Drive. He's planning to remodel the top floor as a penthouse to live in while he keeps an eye on the rest of the building's renovation."

"The old Paramount building?" I ask, trying not to swoon. There's something attractive about a man like Channing taking such a personal interest in his next real estate project. Most men as wealthy as Channing would just let their hired help take the lead on a reno, then step in to collect the profit when it's over. I'm impressed with him already.

"That's the one," Owen continues. He rolls up his sleeves, and the vintage Rolex on his wrist nearly blinds me when the sinking sun hits it just right. He rolls the sleeve back down. "He seemed like a decent guy, and you mentioned that he might be a potential match for Audra, so I invited him here to hang out and surf the shoreline with me a bit this week." He pauses. "And to meet you, of course."

My mind is racing. I've been stalking Channing online for a while now. The man is hot as hell. No reason he couldn't get into a relationship himself. From what I hear, he has plenty of women on his arm, so he clearly has no trouble in that department. Trying out a serious relationship with a woman he's never met might take some cajoling on my part.

When I recently mentioned him to Audra as a potential match, even though I'd never met him in person, she miraculously seemed interested. Which is more than I could say for the dozens of other potential matches I've presented to her recently. She'll be drooling over the idea once I tell her that he's on his way aboard the *MaryLou* for me to potentially audition.

It's a tall order, but my end goal is to pair Audra happily—so I'll do whatever it takes to make it happen.

"Well, cheers to that!" I laugh gleefully, already lost in my thoughts about how to approach Channing later this evening. "How can I get him interested?" I turn toward Owen again, ready to pepper him with questions. They've only shared drinks once, but maybe he has some insight on how I can catch Channing's eye tonight. If I miss this opportunity, Audra might seriously die alone. And, given her powerful network of girlfriends and tabloid connections, we just might have to bury my business right along with her. "What do you think his type is?"

"I think his type is beautiful women," Owen says with a smirk as he stares out at the water. I roll my eyes at him, but he doesn't see it.

"How can I catch his eye tonight?" I ask again, throwing back the rest of my champagne. A deckhand appears to hand us both a refill.

"Well," he starts, turning to face me, but he pauses as his eyes travel down my body. I watch them move south and suddenly everything around us slows down as he takes his time studying me from head to toe. Every last inch of me. I can feel his eyes skimming the thin, silky material I'm wrapped in while it floats between us in the breeze. My skin prickles under his gaze. I hold my breath, waiting for our eyes to meet again.

Owen breaks into a smile when his eyes finally make their way back up to my face. The moment swiftly passes us by as time regains its normal pace. We both awkwardly glance back out toward the sun, nearly under the horizon now. The ship's moody exterior lights have turned on and the soft glow twinkling around us mixes with the fading sun to make this moment feel more intimate than it should be.

He clears his throat.

"Ah, I don't think you'll have any trouble catching his eye tonight, if that's what you're after. I don't know if I've ever seen a man refuse you."

No man except you, I think to myself.

5

By ten p.m., I haven't laid eyes on Channing yet. It's still pretty early by party standards but I'm starting to stress out about his absence on deck. He might have already found someone to share his attention with back in his own stateroom.

The atmosphere here is starting to feel like a playground for the rich and famous. Models, actresses, directors, and more have been flooding the ship all day with the helipad and ferry continually in use. Each guest is more beautiful than the last.

After Owen told me Channing was coming onboard, I'd called Audra back in a quieter part of the ship. She was thrilled when I let her know that Channing would be onboard this week and that I would be working to set them up.

I not-so-accidentally left out the part about me not even laying eyes on him yet. I don't want to let her down again. Especially if this match with Channing doesn't actually take shape.

Audra is amazing, but I can't remember the last time a client frazzled me this fiercely. High-powered needs are part of offering personal services to the world's most successful clientele. Especially when it comes to matters of the heart. And even more especially when it comes to matters *below* the heart. Audra is hanging in there with me, given that her desires in a partner aren't exactly traditional, but I can sense a growing frustration on her end since it's already been three months.

I quickly scan the growing crowd on deck again for Channing's signature five-o'clock shadow and famously chiseled jawline. It's high-time for him to show up, and for me to lay it on thick so I can get him interested in Audra.

The party has grown increasingly rambunctious as guests fill the deck. The tangible stress of their high-octane lifestyles melts off them as more cocktails are poured and the mood of the ship continues to flow into a more carefree state.

A warm Mediterranean breeze whips up periodically whenever another helicopter carries more guests onboard to the ship's helipad, but the volume of Rory's set list is loud enough to mostly drown it out.

Real estate tycoons, runway models, NFL players, oil industry heiresses, Grammy award-winning musicians—all of them are out here celebrating my best friend as he hosts the most epic party of the year. Sometimes I have to pinch myself that this is my real life.

I catch my reflection in one of the ship's grand storm-grade windows. The yellow Prada dress was the right choice for tonight with my thick, platinum hair piled high on my head, thanks to my amazing glam team. Owen's stylist, who I occasionally work with too, suggested I wear the canary diamond drop earrings Owen gave me shortly after he sold his first nanotech company at the end of college.

Looking around the deck, I feel like I can hold my own against the crowd of women here, but I'm ready to get Channing all to myself before any of these other women can make his acquaintance or form any real connections with him. He's going to be a hot commodity out here with his wickedly handsome looks to match his famously thick bank account.

Scanning the deck for Channing again, I spot Shandee, one of the models I met last year at a charity event in Paris. The woman is impossible to miss. She is six-foot-one and unapologetically gorgeous with chocolate-brown skin, and a halo of natural curls.

According to the gossip mill, she's recently single and possibly in need of a match. Shandee's recent record-breaking contract with Dior would make my matchmaking fees look like a drop in the bucket. A group of people around her roar heartily at whatever story she's telling them. She has an outlandish sense of humor and I know I'd be lucky to work with her as a client. Not to mention her social circle of equally successful, beautiful girlfriends that she might refer to me once she's happily matched. Above all else, I'd like to see her happy and in love. The tabloids covering her latest breakup to her ex, Jason, have been brutal.

I start making my way over to her but just as I'm about there, another beautiful woman walks between us and kisses her squarely on the lips. The woman pulls her into an airtight embrace, letting her free arm linger around Shandee's tiny waist, and I'm hit with an unexpected wave of envy. It's been a very long time since someone treated me like that in a genuine way. I push the memories back.

The part of me that was capable of a romantic, meaningful relationship died right along with my interest in spending time out on open water. I haven't let anyone get that close to me since the accident that took everything from me. It's like I've been rewired to live solo. The only person I've been even remotely interested in over the past ten years just so happens to be my best friend. But I won't risk losing him, too.

I smile sadly to myself and take a step back, giving Shandee and her partner more space. I'm happy for her. I only wish that I could open my heart again that way.

Just as I turn to make my way back to Owen, my thoughts are interrupted again by the deafening beat of helicopter blades making their way onboard the ship.

6

As the helicopter touches down, my canary-yellow chiffon dress curls around me, hugging every curve as if it's been tightly superglued to my body. Then it whips out in a long train behind me toward the blackness of the night as the chopper makes the wind pick up. I knew this was the right dress to wear tonight with all the helicopter traffic drumming up a heavy wind.

Some of the models, on the other hand, chose darling little mini dresses. They shriek and laugh each time a helicopter comes in as their shorter hemlines whip up while they struggle to pull them back down like a collection of modern-day Marilyn Monroes strewn out across the deck. The men—and some of the women—out here are loving the show. Most of the models have been clever enough to wear bikinis or thongs underneath.

Curious about who is coming onboard at this hour, I make my way to the side rail to see a tall man with peppered hair climbing out of the helicopter under the blazing spotlights perched alongside the helipad.

I recognize him instantly as one of the wealthiest hedge fund managers in New York City: Mr. Charlie Beckett himself.

He's impeccably dressed and more handsome in person than I've ever seen him appear on a screen. Last I heard, he was single but a bit of a player. More than likely not ready to settle down. To be honest, *a bit of a player* is a generous way of putting it. Like many of Wall Street's finest, he's a trust-fund media darling who always has at *least* one stunning woman on his arm. Which means Charlie is almost definitely not ready for anything serious—a shame because he is absolutely delicious.

For a moment, I think he might have come alone. Probably to sample Owen's stunning guest list of women. But then he whips around after stepping off the aircraft to help a young woman exit the helicopter behind him. Both of them are bent at the waist, ducking over, even though the chopper's blades are spinning too far above their heads to reach them.

I strain my eyes, but I can't make out the woman's face yet. All I can see is a Hermes scarf tied loosely around her bundle of thick, red hair like a 1950s pin-up model. Red tendrils escape the scarf and flap wildly around her head as she and Charlie giggle toward one another and jog to the deckhand who is standing there to greet them with a tray of champagne flutes and martinis.

Her bright red hair and long, willowy frame make me suspect that Charlie's date for the week might be Owen's crush, Cadence Fisher. But it *can't* be. Her attendance here is supposed to be because she has a recent romantic interest in Owen. So why would she be flying in with Charlie? I hope I'm wrong.

Both of them take a glass of Dom from the deckhand, and the woman in the scarf turns to look up at Charlie with a wide, toothy grin as they clink their glasses together. I gasp a little when I finally see her face fully under the lights.

It *is* Cadence Fisher.

I could spot her alabaster complexion—like polished porcelain against her signature red pout—from a mile away. She laughs at something Charlie says, revealing two rows of perfectly blinding teeth against the deep red stain of her lips. She touches his arm and leans against him with the familiarity of a lover, or, I hope, just a friend.

My stomach sinks when I think of Owen's disappointment. As much as it hurts to think of him getting serious with someone else, I really do want him to be happy. I always have. Even if it's not with me.

Charlie turns and motions to another deckhand to take their luggage from the helicopter to their rooms—or room. I make a mental note to find out whether or not they're staying together.

Then they turn and link arms before walking toward the same wing of staterooms.

Well, shit.

Before Owen sees this for himself, I'd like to find out what's really going on so I can break the news to him myself if these two gorgeous specimens did come here romantically. Together. I've heard Cadence is pretty sweet, so a move like this would be uncharacteristically heartless of her. But this crowd of people tend to do whatever they want, feelings of others be damned.

Sometimes I wish Owen would let me set him up with one of my clients, just so I could ensure his happiness with someone who would be perfect for him. Especially if it's not going to be me. But he always says he's not ready. Not yet.

Owen and I have always been painfully platonic. I misread his signals—only once—and tried kissing him back in college. Considering the way that ended, I've regarded that door as being permanently shut. We're both guilty of pretending that kiss from college never happened. Which is mostly my fault, because I'm the one who insisted that I was too drunk to remember it.

Now, as I watch Cadence and Charlie slip into the stairwell to head toward the hallway full of staterooms, I look behind me and spot Owen talking to Shandee. He's telling a story, his arms gesturing out smoothly as Shandee bends at the waist to let out another hearty laugh. Owen is a phenomenal storyteller, self-deprecating and good-natured in all the right places, and a few more guests are joining them now to hear Owen's tale. Everyone roars again, and one of the directors he knows pats him on the back a few times.

Owen must feel me watching him because he pauses when our eyes meet. He winks at me with a sideways grin and a few guests turn to see who he's speaking to silently with only his eyes. Then he cocks his head and nods, beckoning me over to join them.

I hold one finger up and mouth the word *coming* in his direction, before winking back at him with a grin and lightly sighing to myself. Then I make a quick stop at the bar on my way to his group. I'm going to need a drink in my hand before I tell Owen about Cadence's arrival with Charlie Beckett.

35

7

"Coors Light with a lime, please," I say.

The bartender behind the counter—probably in his late twenties—gives me a funny look. "With all this top-shelf liquid courage here, you're really going to order a Coors Light?" He says it like it's a challenge, and I recognize a clear Australian accent over the beat of the music behind us. The bartender's dimples deepen on either side of his mouth when he talks and I can't help but notice the thick rim of black lashes surrounding his light green eyes.

I smile sheepishly at him. Coors Light with lime was Owen's signature drink back at UCLA. He was drinking one the night I kissed him. I could taste the distinct flavor on his lips before he gently turned me away.

"You heard me," I say, allowing a hint of flirtatious sass to infiltrate my voice. He's cute. Actually, he's more than cute.

"Anything for you, gorgeous," he replies and I feel myself start to redden—the warmth spreading low throughout my body. Smooth. No doubt he's raking it in on tips tonight with that smile. Not to mention the rugged accent. And I imagine a few women from this particular crowd might be offering him more than just tips later on.

He pulls out a chilled glass to pour my cheap beer into, but I quickly stop him.

"No, keep it in the bottle," I say.

He laughs and sets the bottle back down on the counter. Then he braces himself against the bar top—white sleeves rolled up to expose two dark rows of tattoos covering each of his arms—and leans toward me with a challenging look. I nod and raise my eyebrows at him, as if to say, *no really, I'd like it in the bottle*.

I reach my hand out to him and crack a smile. "Now, please."

He returns with a good-natured laugh and then shoves two lime slices into the slender neck before handing it to me. Our fingers touch, igniting a quick little spark as I take it from him.

"I prefer it this way," I say with a barely there shrug. He watches as I take a swig from the cold bottle before licking my lips. "Old habits die hard."

The beer mixes with the sour tang of lime bubbling in my mouth as I glance at Owen. I don't know what's come over me—maybe it's the silly flirtation with this hot bartender that has gotten under my skin—but I make sure to catch Owen's eye before taking a second, longer sip. The taste brings back the feeling of his lips touching mine all those years ago. And today is the anniversary of our first kiss, after all. The night of Owen's birthday. I don't know why I still think of it as our first kiss, since there has never been a second.

Owen's jaw hangs open for just a moment when he sees what drink I'm holding.

A slow smile stretches across his face as he shakes his head and runs his fingers through his hair, looking up toward the sky. Then he looks into my eyes again and raises his own glass toward me. A silent toast. His eyes crinkle at the edges and narrow in on me, as if he's asking if I remember.

I know that's just wishful thinking. Still, we seem to be playing a game of cat and mouse with our eyes, even if the game is only in my head.

I take another sip—barely able to contain the bubbling liquid as my lips threaten to part with a smile I can't fully hold back—then I hold the bottle up to meet his private toast. I mouth the word, *cheers,* back at him with a wink, innocently playing the part that I have no idea what this drink might symbolize to him, to us.

Maybe it's this beautiful place, or the adrenaline I'm feeling being out on this enormous ship over open water. But for the first time in years, I'm actually willing him to remember that night. The night I tried crossing the line with our friendship. I still wonder if things might have ended differently if I hadn't pretended to forget what happened between us the next morning.

Whatever the reason, I'm suddenly not afraid of him knowing how I felt about him all those years ago. It's been long enough that maybe we could laugh about it now. At the very least, maybe he'll tell me the reason he pushed me away that night. There's only one way to find out.

And if Cadence is really here with Charlie …

Taking another swig from the bottle, I can practically taste Owen's lips again from that night back in college. It's the push I need to find out. I thank the bartender and hop off my bar stool to start making my way across the deck to join him.

8

Just as I'm making my way over to Owen, a big hand spins me around. I nearly spill the beer in surprise.

I come face-to-chest with a big, barrel-like man. Two enormous biceps strain at the sleeves of his linen shirt. I trace my way up the man's tall, oak-like stature to a pair of light brown eyes and healthy hairline of thick, auburn hair.

I recognize him immediately. It's Texas oil tycoon Coz Webster.

"Coz!" I grin, genuinely happy to see him. I've been vetting him back in the States for my other current VIP client, Zara Cordon. Coz and I have gone on a few PG-rated dinner date auditions. We haven't done anything that might be considered PG-13 yet. But he's passed Zara's list of desires with flying colors, so I have a hunch we'll be sliding into the final stages of his audition process very soon.

When I initially met with Zara over oysters and lemon drops one evening, she had asked me to find her an old-fashioned, traditional man who is wealthier than she is. That man has been tricky to find. Zara owns the wildly popular makeup brand Trixx, and has a carefree, kind personality you don't often find with people at her level of success. She'd told me, "I want a man who's solid. And he has to have rough hands with a few callouses from loving the outdoors. No computer geeks or pencil pushers." I'd laughed at that. Then told her I love when clients give me tiny details that'll turn them on. It makes my job easier to know when I've nailed the right match. At the end of our meeting, after she'd downed three lemon drops and licked the sugared rims, she'd quietly added that she wants an alpha-type who will treat her like a lady everywhere else but the bedroom. "I want him to toss me around a little," she'd nearly whispered and blushed after saying the last part out loud. I assured her that I hear the same thing from most of my clients. They all want a perfect gentleman who will rip their clothes off behind closed doors.

I haven't tested this particular desire of Zara's out on Coz yet, but from the way he's looking me up and down now, I have a feeling that he won't disappoint when I do.

"Well, hello there, Cher." Coz eyes me with appreciation. I can tell he's already had a drink or two because his Southern accent tends to deepen after he's knocked back a few. But, like all of the guests on the ship, he's just here to enjoy himself. We've all flown halfway across the world for a week like this. "Fancy seeing you here, darlin'! Although I figured I might run into you this week considering you and Owen are a package deal back at home."

I smile but don't comment. Many of our mutual friends see Owen and me as a closet couple since we're always together.

And sometimes my potential matches are hesitant of ruining their relationship with Owen if I carry out a full audition on them. I often have to reassure them that Owen isn't going to care about what we do together behind closed doors. No matter how much I wish that he would.

"What's the deal with you two, anyway?" he asks. There it is. Right on cue. "Closet lovers? Secret romancières?"

"Oh, you know I'm eternally single and not in the market for myself, Coz." I roll my eyes at him. "And you need to squash that silly rumor the next time you hear it. Owen and I have always been just boring old friends-without-benefits."

I stifle a wince as I glance at Owen and see that he's still watching me from across the deck. The memory of his lips on mine hits again when I take another sip of my beer, letting the fizzy liquid tingle on my tongue before swallowing. Then I turn back to Coz.

"As long as you're sure you're single." Coz lightly brushes my hair off my shoulder.

"I am," I say, "and so is the VIP client I have in mind for you. I assume you're still looking for something serious?"

I watch his body language carefully. He definitely meets Zara's height requirement, standing six-foot-six and towering over me in my Louboutin stiletto sandals. But I need to know if he's interested in what Zara wants.

Coz nods. "Oh, of course. Just sayin'. If I was Owen, I would have snatched you right up years ago. Y'all are wastin' your time if you're not knockin' boots at least a third of the time you're together ..." He trails off as a tiny young waitress tries to maneuver her way around his muscular frame, but she misses her mark, accidentally knocking her empty tray into one of his boulder-like shoulders. He swings around to face her, a flash of irritation on his face.

"Oh, excuse me, miss," he says, realizing it's just an embarrassed young woman trying to get around him. He immediately dips into a slight bow to let her pass. She giggles before gathering herself, then scurries away to go fill her tray again. When he turns back to me, I realize he's wearing his cowboy boots like he's still in Texas. Except he's on a yacht in Saint-Tropez. I seize it as my opportunity to change the subject away from Owen and me.

"Boots on a boat, Coz?" I say with a smirk, gesturing to his worn leather boots that would be a better fit for a cattle roundup than a luxurious yacht party on the Mediterranean Sea.

He chuckles when he looks down. "They help keep my sea legs attached to my body out here." He grins back at me. His boots must be size sixteen or more. The man is enormous.

I feel a stir in my gut as I wonder what else is enormous about him.

Contrary to some of the more unsultry rumors about my business, I don't just jump into bed with any man that I would consider to be a potential match for my VIPs. Quite a bit of background checking has to happen first, courtesy of Daisy, along with a few audition conversations or dates. My client also has to be fully informed and onboard with the match before I'll finish off the final step. I'm something of an expert at reading body language and extracting a wealth of information from the most casual questions. And, most importantly, I have to be satisfied by what he brings to the table sexually. If he can't create chemistry with me, then why would they be able to successfully seduce my client?

Fortunately for my business, but unfortunately for me, I excel at completely turning off any part of myself that feels the slightest hint of an emotional romance with a match as their matchmaker. Every time I have sex as part of a Full 360 Audition, it's a pure joy ride. No truly intimate feelings. Nothing more than business casual. Keeping everything unemotional, no strings attached, is the number-one rule I have for myself.

"Can I get you a drink?" Coz is staring down at my beer bottle.

I hold up the bottle, still about half full.

"I mean a *real* drink," he says, laughing. "I thought you were more of a top-shelf bubbly kind of girl. But if you're more into cheap beer ..." He trails off with a laugh.

I glance behind him and see Owen is talking to three women who look like they just stepped off a runway in Milan. One of them has her hand resting on his shoulder.

"On second thought, yes to another drink," I say to Coz and see him perk up.

9

I can't ask Owen about our college kiss with those three gorgeous girls distracting him right now. And if Channing isn't going to show up on deck tonight, I may as well make the most of my time with Coz. I could use a good distraction. Plus, it'd be helpful to get him off my roster and moved on to Zara so I can focus solely on finding a match for Audra this week.

"What do you suggest for a drink?" I ask him.

Resting against his forearm, he leads me back to the bar where the green-eyed Aussie bartender is still serving drinks. Everything about Coz is rock solid and screams big, southern gentleman. He's one of the old-money oil tycoons Owen has done business with in the past, and his net worth engulfs Zara's sizable sum. I smile to myself as he makes casual banter with me while we work our way through the crowd. Coz just might be perfect for Zara.

He slides his arm out of my hands and wraps it around my shoulders when we arrive at the bar. His big hand against my back feels nice. It's helping me forget the three things I'd rather forget at this moment: The fact that I'm on a ship, the three women hovering around Owen, and the white lie I fed Audra earlier tonight about Channing already being interested in getting matched.

The bartender gives me another gorgeous smile when Coz and I walk up together. "Change your mind about that one there, love?" he says, nodding down toward my half-empty beer bottle, which is now dripping wet condensation onto my hand.

I put the bottle on the bar and wipe my hand with a black cocktail napkin he gives me. He flashes me a confident grin that comes dangerously close to an I-told-you-so smirk. It makes me laugh.

"This handsome man here has insisted on getting me a *real* drink." I nod up at Coz coyly. I can tell he's really working hard to push this audition forward. Zara is a great catch. He'd be lucky to end up with her, but I can't say that I'm not enjoying his attention as we continue flirting in front of the bartender— who seems to be enjoying the spectacle himself. Coz's larger-than-life personality plays like a magnet to those around him. He knows we're giving the bartender a good show as he gets to work drawing me in.

"So, tell me more about what Zara is looking for," Coz says, shifting his body toward mine so we're just inches apart. Close enough that his body heat warms my bare shoulders when I lean in to hear him. I can smell the familiar bergamot notes of his Creed Aventus cologne—a favorite among many of the men I audition. It smells expensive.

"I think we covered most of that during our last dinner back in Malibu," I remind him.

"Oh, I remember," he breathes the words out confidently, "but there were a few things we didn't get to discuss in public." His eyes slowly leave mine and travel down my neck, falling to the edge of my dress—the part that skims across my chest. He's so sure of himself. I feel a little shiver travel down my spine as I pick up a bit of a take-charge vibe in him. Zara will love this more intense, sexy side of him.

"If I'm not mistaken, I think we've hit four out of five of Zara's must-haves." His eyes are pouring into mine now and I can hear the suggestive tone in his voice. I feel my pulse quicken. "Have I filled all your checkboxes yet?"

God, I love my job.

"Well, I already know you're very successful," I start to say. The bartender puts our drinks on the countertop. "Thank you," I say to him as Coz hands me my drink.

"Check," Coz says, tucking a strand of hair behind my ear. It sends goosebumps down my arms.

"And I know your personality is … all right," I tease him.

"Check," he says slowly, but furrows his brow. "Just all right?"

"I'd say more than all right." I laugh. "But only just." I take a sip of the drink I've been handed and let my tongue purposefully linger on the slender straw, then I grip it between my teeth with a smile before releasing it again.

Coz tilts his head back and erupts with a hearty, energetic laugh that makes the bartender and the couple next to us turn and look at us like they want in on the joke too. He takes a tiny step toward me so his body heat is drifting through the thin layer of my dress—all the way down the length of my body.

I could easily take him tonight. Finish our audition, and then I'll hand him off to Zara in the morning.

"Remind me of what else Zara is looking for," he says to me more suggestively.

"Loyalty," I say. "A future." This catches him a bit off guard. I see him falter, if only for a moment before he regains his composure.

He locks eyes with me again. "I'm ready to settle down. If something were to happen between you and I tonight, it would be my last rodeo. Then I'd let Miss Zara make an honest man out of me, if the chemistry is right. I want children. A family."

I can see he's telling the truth.

"Check," I say agreeably.

"What else?"

"I know there's one more thing she was asking for …" I pretend to be confused, like I can't remember the final major ask on Zara's list.

"Can I help you remember, by chance?" he asks. His free hand reaches for mine and he starts to run his thumb over my wrist. Rough calluses line his palm, landing just below each Texas-sized finger that engulfs my smaller hand in his.

"You can try," I say, "but you should know that I'm a hands-on learner." I love that he's taking control of where the night is headed, seducing me like he would with Zara.

He lets loose with that larger-than-life laugh again and the bartender looks up at us with a funny look on his face. Like he has watched thousands of men and women cross that threshold of attraction throughout his bartending career and knows exactly what it looks like when the moment of consent takes shape. But this isn't it yet.

We're almost there.

I lean into Coz and speak just loudly enough so that I know he can hear me. I'm enjoying the fact that the bartender is watching this play out too. "If we spend time together tonight, it'll be the final step of your audition for Zara," I say, not holding back my intentions. I make sure I'm crystal clear about what's going to happen next, so there's no confusion. This is going to be fun for both of us, but it's not about *us*. It's a one-night-only audition on behalf of my client, and that point has to be clear before we can ever start crossing the line.

"For Zara," he says as he pulls back so I can see his face full-on when he says it.

I study him for a moment. "For Zara," I finally say, clinking my glass against his in agreement.

"Your room or mine?" he asks. This makes me laugh.

The bartender suddenly seems to choke on something, and I look at him pointedly with a grin. I'm positive that he's never seen a negotiation quite like ours before. He's amused, I can tell, but he laughs to himself, then clears his throat and shakes his head as if to say, "Believe me, I've seen it all."

I glance up at Coz.

"Yours," I say simply.

I give the Aussie a wink as Coz slides a hand around my shoulder and starts leading me across the deck.

The speakers are pumping the unmistakable beat of the band's latest ballad and the party guests begin to whoop and holler, dancing to the music.

We make our way toward the hallway that leads to a collection of staterooms, and I look over my shoulder just in time to catch Owen shifting his gaze away from me as he turns to greet the man next to him with a warm handshake.

I keep my eyes on him until I reach the edge of the darkened hall. He steals a glance at me just as Coz and I duck inside.

10

I sit down on the edge of a leather smoking chair next to the fireplace in Coz's stateroom. It's smaller than my room, but furnished beautifully with the same understated elegance the entire ship was designed with.

The gas fireplace is on and flames are glittering across the blue crystal rocks lining the base of the fire. It reminds me of the waves sparkling under the fiery sunset that Owen and I shared earlier tonight. I start unbuckling one of my stilettos, trying not to dwell on the memory of Owen's face as we watched the sun sink lower. His eyes traveling down my body—carefully studying every part of me like he could actually see underneath my dress as the sun disappeared under the horizon—

"Okay, so how does this final part of the audition work?" Coz's question snaps me back to the present.

"Didn't you get the birds-and-bees talk, Coz?" I say with a smile. Obviously I'm joking, but I feel the need to break the ice a bit now that we're alone. I'm not going to initiate anything from here on out. I need him to take charge and show me how tonight is going to go. But first I need to get these heels off. I slip one foot out of my Louboutins and stretch my toes, shifting in the chair to reach my foot toward the warmth of the fire beside me. I try to imagine we're in Coz's bedroom back in Texas on dry land—instead of suspended over the Mediterranean Sea.

"You can keep those on if you'd like," he says in a husky voice, gesturing to the other stiletto still strapped to my ankle. He's watching me from his position near the foot of the bed.

"Oh, I see how it is." I laugh. Clearly, watching me remove my shoes, or keep them on, is all part of this experience for him. Curious, I sit back and hold my foot up to him: A silent invitation for him to help me remove the stiletto, if that's what he wants. Coz moves to kneel on the floor in front of me by the fire. Even kneeling, his stature is still imposing. Everything about his size makes me feel small next to him.

He slips my other shoe off and envelopes my foot in a warm massage. I enjoy the gentle strength of him as he works each tight muscle in my arch to release all the tension brought on by those four-inch heels.

Zara will appreciate this more nurturing side of him. I have yet to see his inner tiger come out, but I have a feeling I'm about to.

"Do you have a thing for feet or shoes?" I ask, turning all of my attention to him.

"Both," he says as his hands start working their way up the curve of my ankle. "Mostly I have a thing for beautiful women and everything about them." He's earnest when he says it, and his eyes drift up from where his hands are sliding down my foot and lock in my gaze. I allow myself to relax into the calming feel of his touch against my skin.

I need this, as much for myself as to match Zara. To be touched in a way that helps me forget everything else around me. And I can already tell Coz is going to be good with his hands.

Check.

The warmth of his palms spreads up the length of my body. He reaches up toward my knee, then back down the muscle of my calf, drawing down to the curve of my ankle and back up again.

Sighing appreciatively, I crack open my eyes just wide enough to notice how the bulge of his biceps work with each pump of his arm while he moves his hands against my bare skin. I'm auditioning him for Zara, but that goes hand-in-hand with soaking up every bit of pleasure tonight while I make sure I've found a man who won't disappoint her.

He catches me eyeing him and I smile back. This angle—with him down there and me up here on the chair—is seducing us both.

"Time for the other side?" he asks but doesn't wait for a reply before moving his hands to my other foot. My lips curve up a little more and I sit up higher so I can watch his body respond to mine.

"Are you keeping those on?" I ask, eyeing his soft, calf-skin boots still planted firmly on his feet. But he sits back on the floor without taking his eyes off me to slip the boots to the floor.

While he continues massaging me, he adds little kisses on the tip of each of my toes. At first, his lips barely brush against my skin. Then he slows down, running his mouth up my ankle. He's testing the waters, going a little higher. And higher still.

With each passing second, he slowly travels up my body, closer toward my dress's hemline. I can't wait to see how he takes control of my body and I'm stuck between wanting to make this moment—and the feeling of his mouth against my bare skin—last a bit longer, while also wanting to jump off my chair to straddle him right now in front of the crackling firelight. My skin percolates under his touch but I force myself to just sit still. I'm not here to take him quickly. I need to know what he can do for me—and for Zara, so I let him take his time.

I grip the leather chair as he runs his tongue along my knee. Then he kisses my thigh, pausing long enough to pull his shirt up over his head, revealing a row of tightly strung ab muscles. He presses his warm body against my legs as he kisses my thigh. Skin against skin—velvety and smooth.

I slide my knees open to hug his torso, feeling more of his skin warm mine as he pushes his body closer, still kneeling before me. His eyes are now level with mine. Then he wraps both arms around me—each bicep as wide as my waist—and effortlessly pulls me to the edge of my seat so our bodies can fully press together. I sit up straighter, pushing my hips against his chest—chiffon against chiseled muscle.

He kisses me on the lips just once before pulling back an inch to speak. "You're wearing entirely too much clothing, Miss Thatcher." His breath tickles my ear, sending a shockwave down the length of my body, settling into the part of me that's leaning hungrily into his torso. I'm aching for him to kiss me again—anywhere he wants. But instead, he lingers near my mouth. We both pant while his hands continue exploring up and down my legs. His lips grin against mine when my breath catches in my throat.

I hug his chest tighter with my thighs as he slides his hands up the curve of my legs—higher than before—while he watches my face. I try to kiss him on the mouth to break our eye contact, but he doesn't allow it. He pulls back slightly to watch my eyes as he glides his hands up under the hem of my dress, along my hips. His gaze locks with mine, and I fight the urge to close my eyes in delight as he skims my lace thong with his thumbs. Then he pulls the edges of my panties back with two fingers. He plays along my skin underneath while he holds me firmly in place—my legs on either side of him with his mouth just out of reach of my own.

It feels incredibly intimate for him to explore me like this while he watches me respond to his touch. But instead of closing the gap between us with a kiss, I follow his lead because I'm here to find out how well he can take charge of a woman's body. He's enjoying his dominance over me as his hands explore me more without giving me exactly what I want. And it's pushing me to relinquish all of my control to him as I move my hips farther into his hands. The man knows exactly what he's doing. He reaches around to my ass and squeezes hard. I groan, and he finally covers my mouth with his. He kisses me slowly at first, then more urgently as I open my mouth to him. He pulls me in closer to his body so I can finally feel his erection through his pants, pushing against my wet panties. Then he stands abruptly, lifting me from the chair in one quick movement.

He grips my ass while I straddle him, squeezing him with my legs still wrapped around him as he carries me across the room. He stops kissing me long enough to toss me down across the bed. I push back on my elbows to watch him unbutton his pants, then try not to gasp when his boxers fall to the floor. Zara is going to be a very lucky woman.

But me first.

He firmly pulls my panties all the way off with one hand and crawls between my knees and starts dragging his tongue up my leg. When he gets to the softness of my inner thigh, he brings my hips toward him. I close my eyes when I feel his hot breath against my crotch and pull my dress above my hips, silently inviting him to take whatever he wants.

"Look at me." His voice cuts through the sound of our ragged panting. "I want to see your face when I kiss you right here."

I will myself to obey and open my eyes to watch him kiss the mound between my thighs slowly while his eyes stay on mine. He kisses me once. Then twice. We hold eye contact as he pulls my knees farther apart and his tongue explores every open inch of me.

"Fuck, Coz," I breathe out. Knowing a man has to please me fully in order to be matched with one of my clients means that I usually get to enjoy the best fuck of their life.

He slips one finger, then two inside me now, letting his tongue work everywhere around me except the one place I want to feel it the most. I grip the sheets so hard, my nails burn as he pushes my knees toward my chest.

"Please, Coz," I whisper, barely audible against his ruthless teasing. "Please."

He takes all of me into his mouth as a rush of starbursts fill my vision. I'm not quite there yet, but I'm quickly approaching the edge.

"Condom?" I ask with urgency.

"One step ahead of you," he says, then continues working his mouth as I hear the quiet rip of a wrapper and feel his body shift. Then, as if he's read my mind, he adds, "But we're not there yet."

Suddenly he pulls his mouth away from me and moves onto the bed to hover above me. In the light of the fire, I can see every inch of him now. Naked muscle rippling against the firelight. Every bit of him is hard and tight in all the best places. Then his erection pushes into me and I lift my hips to meet his. We move together, while his eyes dig deeper into mine. In and out as he kisses the soft skin under my ear, and back up to watch my face again. Just as I'm about to fall over the edge, he releases me and I feel him move down the bed. My eyes spring open in time to see him start licking and kissing between my legs for a second time as he pushes my knees apart with his hand. Then he replaces his erection inside me with his fingers. I ride against them and his mouth at the same time.

"Coz, I'm not going to last." I somehow manage to breathe out the words as I look into his eyes, begging him to take me over the cliff into ecstasy. I'm completely at his mercy as he expertly slows everything down to the point that I'm pulsing at his every touch. "Please," I whisper. Then he thrusts his erection between my legs again, filling me once more while he nips my skin gently at the nape of my neck. It's too much to handle. In two more thrusts, we both come, sweaty and panting, sending shockwaves down every limb.

"Holy shit, Coz," I moan into the pillow next to me. This is what fucking dreams are made of and Zara is going to die over this man's performance in bed.

Check.

Both of us are completely out of breath. "Holy shit, Coz," I say again. It's all I can think to say. I've auditioned a lot of men, but this was one of the best 360s I've had the pleasure of enjoying so far.

"Good enough to pass?" He grins at me, still panting. He knows he's just completely rocked my world, and, in turn, his audition for Zara.

"Fuck," I breathe out. He smiles and leans in to kiss my bare shoulder.

"You're not so bad yourself," he murmurs. I close my eyes and laugh. He's just owned me entirely. And I know I've just hit the nail on the head when it comes to matching him with Zara. She's going to be thrilled.

As my breathing slows and my heartbeat returns to normal, I slowly roll off the bed and straighten my dress—slipping my panties into my purse to make the short walk back to my own stateroom.

"That was amazing," I say, smiling down at Coz, who looks like a Greek god still sprawled out across the length of the bed we've just shared. "You'll be hearing from my assistant for date details when we have everything set up for you and Zara."

"That's it?" he says. "Not one for a cuddle afterward? Maybe a second quickie once we both recover?"

I squeeze his shoulder then let my hand linger on his cheek before turning toward the door.

"You know this was strictly business, Coz," I say. I'm always careful to remind my matches that this is all part of the Full 360 Audition process, every step of the way. But sometimes in the afterglow of a good fuck they'll forget. "You passed. No need for another go."

"You're welcome to sleep it off in here," he persists, still lying across the bed. There's a slight glimmer of hurt in his eyes. I open the door a few inches, then turn back to face him full-on so he pays more attention to what I'm saying this time.

"Strictly business, Coz," I repeat. "But I'll let Zara know that you were magnificent." He smiles at this, so I take it as my cue to slip out into the hall, letting the door close gently behind me.

Right away, I bump into someone behind me.

"Whoops!" I say at the same time I hear a man's voice utter, "Uh, excuse me."

I spin around to see the wickedly handsome Channing Stanbury staring right back at me.

11

He's even hotter in person than I thought he'd be. And impeccably dressed in a pair of tailored navy slacks with a white Gucci button-up loosened around his neck. He could have just walked off a GQ cover shoot.

"Channing?" His name is out of my mouth before I can stop it.

He eyes me suspiciously for a beat too long.

"And you are …?" he replies. He's watching me intently, probably wondering how a stranger in a dimly lit hallway in the middle of Saint-Tropez knows who he is.

I'm trying to come up with a reply that doesn't sound like *I've been stalking you online*, when I hear the door creak open behind me. Coz is standing in the doorway wearing nothing but a bed sheet wrapped loosely around his waist.

I spin around, horrified. Channing looks at Coz, then at the pair of Louboutins hanging from my fingertips. It won't help, but I immediately bring a hand up to smooth down my hair. I heavily suspect that it's a total mess after that romp.

Coz breaks the silence first.

"Channing!" Coz greets him heartily. I step aside as he removes one hand from his bedsheet and holds it out to Channing.

Still eyeing me cautiously, Channing takes Coz's hand and shakes it. He looks from Coz to me and back to Coz. I close my eyes and try not to cringe when I remember where Coz's hand has just been.

"Do you know Cher Thatcher?" Coz releases Channing's hand and motions toward me. "This here is the queen of elite matchmaking back in the States."

Channing looks at me with an amused expression on his face. This is not how I wanted to meet him. Not at all. My name tends to precede me. But regardless of whether he knows who I am or not, this is going to give him the wrong impression of me and my business right from the start.

"Nice to meet you." I collect myself and manage to flash him a confident smile. I'm not ashamed about what Coz and I have just done. But this is definitely not how I wanted to meet Channing Stanbury this week—with my hair a mess as I make a little walk of shame back to my room. I silently curse Coz for not staying put in his room instead of chasing me out into the hallway.

"Oh, Owen's famous friend Cher?" he asks. At least he looks satisfied with this explanation of why I seem to know who he is. Owen must have mentioned me to him while they were having drinks. I bite my bottom lip and wonder what else Channing already knows about me.

"The one and only!" I manage to reply with a lopsided smile. I'm still trying to smooth out my hair, but my fingers keep getting caught in tangled knots.

"Nice to meet you," he says, stifling a smirk. He holds out his hand and I have to shift the heels to the crook of my arm to shake it. Mortifying. "I'm Channing, but it seems like you already know that." I bite my tongue, but let him finish. "I was just making my way down to the party, but … maybe it's already over?" he says, glancing down at the sheet wrapped around Coz's waist, then to the shoes dangling from my fingertips.

I have to concentrate hard to not roll my eyes at him. His arrogance is, against my better judgment, oddly attractive. But there's something different about him that's making my stomach flip in knots. Something raw. Whatever spark keeps igniting between us as we make eye contact is making me feel like I don't ever want him to walk away from me.

"This party's never over." I smile, trying desperately to sound witty, but I probably look like a deer caught in headlights. A deer with bad hair and underwear in her purse.

"Clearly," he says, looking between us again, laughing.

A zap of electricity runs down my body when our eyes meet again and I'm instantly blushing against my will. I don't know if he has this effect on every woman he meets, but there's a little joke playing across his lips that I can't quite put my finger on. Whether it's his pheromones mixing in the air with mine, or his ridiculous good looks—whatever it is, I can see why he has a legendary reputation with the ladies. He might be a bit arrogant, but he's magnetic as hell.

"But please, don't let me keep you," he says. "It was nice to meet you." He glances down at my bare feet, and I feel that electric tingle again.

"Likewise," I say, hoping my cheeks aren't as red as they feel. I just had a satisfying romp with Coz, but I could seriously shove Channing through the open door behind us and have a second go. In fact, sex with Coz feels like foreplay compared to what I'd like to be doing with Channing right now.

He turns to Coz. "Catch you later. You two enjoy your, um …" He pauses, his face curling into a devilishly handsome grin, and I nearly melt into the floor. "Uh, you two enjoy your evening. Or what's left of it anyway." He pats me playfully on the shoulder as he walks past and I fight the urge to follow him. Instead I close my eyes and exhale one long stream of air.

Auditioning Channing to the fullest extent would be my favorite kind of night. I'd love to be the reason a man like that goes weak in the knees. To watch his face as he lets everything go. And see the weaker side of him after he's just been completely and utterly destroyed by me. I haven't felt such an intense pull to anyone like this since, well, possibly ever.

Channing disappears down the hall toward the thumping music on deck. He's sure to meet an endless supply of beautiful women vying to make his acquaintance tonight. I'm not sure what to make of him yet, but based on our first interaction I can tell why he's always labeled as an international playboy in the tabloids. He's the type of man where a simple look in your direction with those intense eyes of his will make you forget your own name. Add that wicked grin, and all bets are off.

He could easily have his pick of any supermodel or actress on deck. Probably three or four at a time if that's what he's into. Is there any chance he's interested in settling down with Audra? She's beautiful, successful, and incredibly put-together—like all my clients. But she's not exactly a walk in the park. How am I supposed to convince him to audition with me this week for a real-life relationship when he's surrounded by an endless supply of flings?

"Goodnight, Channing," I sigh after him, though he's probably out of earshot. So instead, I turn back to Coz who's still eyeing me gleefully from the doorway. "And goodnight, Coz," I add firmly.

"Not ready for round two?" he asks.

"No," I say, now deeply annoyed. There's an edge to my voice I realize, but I'm frustrated that he didn't listen to what I told him earlier: that his audition is over now and forever. Yes, we just had mind-blowing sex, but it was only to match him with Zara. "There won't be a round two, Coz. You know that."

Clingers do happen occasionally when it comes to auditions. And Coz is starting to show some major red flags to join the ranks as a stage-five clinger. I'll need to pass him over to Zara as quickly as I can. If he keeps this up, there won't be a match at all.

"My assistant Daisy will be in touch to set up your introduction to Zara soon," I remind him more gently. I need to focus on my biggest goal of the week. And that goal just walked down the hall.

I catch a glimpse of myself in the gold-framed mirror at the end of the hallway.

Wonderful. Lipstick and mascara are smeared on my face ever so slightly, and my hair is still tossed wildly in a few places. The edge of my nude thong is hanging out the top of my Chanel handbag, which I hadn't even noticed until now. I look like a sorority girl venturing out on her walk of shame the morning after a big party.

But I manage to smile at myself in the mirror anyway and wipe the smeared corner of lipstick off with the back of my other hand while still holding my shoes. At least I've made contact with Channing. Even if it wasn't ideal, it's a start. And I can work with that.

Coz starts to say something else from down the hall, but I'm not in the mood.

"Goodbye, Coz," I say flatly without turning around.

12

"Room service!"

A knock on the door abruptly pulls me out of the dream I was having. In my dream state, I was happily back on land in Malibu with my Bengal cat, Sonny—both of us drinking water from his bowl on the floor with a straw. It was weirdly comforting.

"You can leave the tray outside," I call back, half asleep. Then I grab my phone off the nightstand. I want to check in on Sonny using my PetCam app, but there are already two missed calls from Audra popping up on the screen. I groan and hit *ignore*, then pull up the live feed of my little Bengal instead. A pet-sitting service is staying with him at my penthouse, but I like looking in at what he's doing every day. Right now, I can see his sleek, leopard-spotted form napping in a puddle of sunshine.

I hear another knock on the door.

"Rooooooom service!" the voice calls out again, this time higher-pitched.

I recognize that voice. It's Owen giving me his best *Mrs. Doubtfire* impression. We watched the movie together once back in college. No doubt he's standing on the other side of my door holding a big tray of breakfast that he likely stole from one of the deck hands.

Throwing back the heavy down comforter, I smile to myself and snatch a robe off the back of a nearby chair as I make my way across the room to let him in. Having breakfast first thing in the morning together whenever we travel is kind of our thing. He knows I never stay the whole night with anyone I audition, so he can always find me in my bed first thing.

The door clicks open before I can get to it. Like I pictured, Owen is waiting outside my door with a breakfast tray filled with fresh fruit, green juice, and delicate French pastries. My room attendant took our orders for breakfast yesterday before the rest of the evening's festivities got underway.

"You really need to keep this door locked," he says when I can see his face. "Too many drunks on the ship this week who might stumble into an open door like this and see it as an invitation."

"Good morning to you too," I say, ignoring the rest of his comment. "How was your first night on the ship, birthday boy?"

"You know, that's the second time your door has been unlocked this week," he points out, ignoring my question as he walks in. I roll my eyes at him. Always the protective big brother figure. I secretly wish *he'd* get drunk and lose his inhibitions before visiting my unlocked room later.

Owen sets the tray of food down on my stateroom's long dining table, then presses the button on the wall panel to make the wall of blackout curtains retract like a synchronized dance. I blink as my eyes adjust to see the morning sunlight sparkling off deep blue waves outside.

My stomach churns. I'm not sure I'll ever be able to appreciate that view of open water.

Breathe, I remind myself. *It's just water.*

A gentle swell crests, carrying a bit of seaweed floating on it.

And that's all it takes for the churning in my stomach to intensify into a full-blown flashback. Suddenly, it's like I'm right back there in the water, my head breaking the surface. Bits of wreckage churning around me while I try to scream.

I can practically feel the icy-cold water immersing my body as I breathlessly grip the chair in front of me.

"Hey …" I hear Owen say gently, his voice cutting through the horror. "Are you okay?"

My body is trembling, but Owen is standing beside me with his arm tucked around my ribcage.

"I'm okay," I insist, trying to hide the fact that I'm shivering. "Just … a little flashback." I'm officially shook. I haven't had a flashback in a long time. I learned from my counselor that they can be wildly unpredictable. They were bad those first few years. I'd be fine one minute, then traveling back to the worst moment of my life the next. And the simplest things would trigger them. Like that bit of seaweed out there, floating on a wave.

"I know you said you wanted to come out here for the week. I thought since it's been so long …" He trails off, still eyeing me. I ease my grip on the back of the chair and force myself to breathe more slowly. "But maybe it's still too soon?"

Just the feel of his body supporting me brings my heart rate back down. In the months after the accident, Owen was there for me more than anyone else in the world. When I dropped out of college—my final semester—he insisted that I live in his guest room while I recovered emotionally and physically from the trauma. This little flashback is nothing compared to what he's seen me go through.

"No, no, I'm fine," I say firmly, looking away from the water and back to the breakfast tray. My eyes land on a glass of green juice and I throw the celery garnish aside to take a big gulp, hoping the cold liquid will stop the nausea that's starting to churn in my gut. "I wanted to be here." I didn't choose this location to celebrate his birthday party on a whim. I know how much he loves it out here, and it felt like one step closer toward enjoying what I used to love: being out on the water.

"I know how much you miss them. I miss them too," he says into my hair and kisses the top of my head again. He continues to hold me while I take a shaky breath into his chest and turn my face toward the water again, this time steadying myself against his sturdy frame.

He leans down and pulls me into a hug while my body responds by letting go a little more. I always fit into his arms like I was meant to be there. Like two pieces of a puzzle that fit perfectly when held together.

Owen gave me all the space and time I needed to grieve right after the accident. Which for me meant hardly getting dressed and waiting until he left on business trips to cry as loud as I needed—often echoing into the empty walls of his house. It was in the months following the accident that he, more than anyone else, helped put what was left of me back together.

"Thank you," I say, allowing myself to stare beyond the balcony into the shimmering Mediterranean Sea again. Practice makes everything better, I remind myself. "But really, I'm fine. And matchmaking is the perfect distraction from the fact that we're floating on this little dinghy."

Owen laughs, looking relieved. Breaking away from him, I grab a banana off the tray to accompany the juice, then settle back into the chair. He slowly circles my back with his knuckles a few times before swiping an apple from the tray and grabbing the seat next to me at the table. He can tell when I don't want to dwell on the subject, or need a good distraction.

"Speaking of work," he says. "I saw you heading out of the party last night with Coz Webster."

"Good eye," I say, biting into the banana and continuing to stare pointedly at the horizon. Exposure therapy at its finest. "He's officially matched with Zara." I glance up at him in time to see him raise his eyebrows back at me. Owen knows that when a match is complete, we've more than likely been intimate.

"And how was he?" he asks. There's a hint of something in his voice, but I can't tell what it is. Owen knows how much work goes into vetting these men before I spend any significant time with them alone—and he's incredibly supportive of my career at this point. I share more juicy details with him than with clients, sometimes.

"He was fine," I say. I'm being nonchalant, but I can't stop a slow smile creeping across my face as I remember the intimate details from my time with Coz last night.

"Just fine?" Owen laughs watching me. "I think your face says that he was more than fine."

"Oh my god, Owen. I didn't know mouths could move like that," I breathe out—lost again in the memory of last night. Coz annoyed me after we had sex, but the sex—*oh my god*—the sex was so good.

"You really do have the best job." He laughs as I'm pulled out of my trance with a sheepish grin.

"I really do," I reply absently, lost in thought. "I also met Channing last night," I add, shifting my eyes back to Owen's.

"Channing Stanbury?" he asks.

"No, Channing Tatum," I tease, rolling my eyes at him before taking another mouthful of banana. Owen leans over and takes a bite off the top of my banana. I push him away playfully as I watch him chew. "Channing seemed kind of–"

I can't find the right word to describe Channing, because I'm not sure what the vibe between us was all about quite yet.

"Prickly?" he fills in for me.

"*Intense*, actually, I'd say. Maybe arrogant? Intriguing, for sure. He saw me coming out of Coz's room last night on his way out to the party deck." Owen stops chewing and widens his eyes at me.

"Not the introduction you were hoping for?" he jokes, reading my mind.

"Right? I felt like I'd been caught coming out of the boys' bathroom at a high school dance," I admit. Even now, I can feel myself turning red again. Both from the awkwardness and the intense pull I felt toward him during that brief meeting. I shake off the memory.

"I think Channing is the type that needs a bit of time to warm up to new people," Owen says thoughtfully. "At least that was my impression of him when we got drinks back in LA together."

I try to imagine Channing and Owen sitting at a bar together, just shooting the shit and trying to get to know each other, but it doesn't sit right with me. I can't see them becoming friends right away. Maybe ever. Owen's laidback, west-coast vibe can meld with just about anyone, but Channing is all east-coast swagger. And sharp as a knife.

"Catching his attention this week might be trickier than I was hoping," I murmur to myself. Then, remembering who else I saw last night, I slowly add, "Oh, I saw Cadence come onto the ship late last night." I pause so I can watch his face before saying the next part. "She was with Charlie Beckett."

"I heard," Owen says, grabbing his own mixture of thick, green juice off the tray. He takes a long sip, staring out at the sea's horizon before continuing. I notice a bit of tension in his jaw.

"I didn't see that one coming," he admits. "I invited Cadence and Charlie separately, but I guess they decided to come together. Never got the chance to talk to her last night. They might have just stayed in their rooms—or room?—after coming in late. Plenty of fish in the sea though, right?" He smiles at me then takes another sip, crunching an ice cube between his teeth. I hate it when he does that.

"You're going to crack your teeth," I say while nudging him with my foot under the table, but he keeps chewing without looking at me. If the issue with Cadence is bothering him, he doesn't seem to want to talk about it more. For a moment, I think about bringing up our kiss. But in the bright sunlight—and without the liquid courage of last night—I lose my nerve and change the subject.

"Well then, if Cadence is off the table, are you ready to let me match you with one of my clients?" I ask with a grin. Occasionally I'll shoot him this question. Mostly it's so I can feel out whether or not he's feeling ready for a serious relationship with someone.

He laughs and sets the glass down, turning to give me his full attention—his eyes playfully narrowing back at me.

13

"That would require one of your famous auditions, wouldn't it?" Owen says in a measured tone, but those crystal eyes of his suddenly sparkle like the latest set of waves rolling in outside. My mouth hangs open for a beat before I can respond. Instant warmth spreads down my legs, filling everything in between, and suddenly I'm pulsing with every heartbeat. Just like that, this man can make me go weak with just the thought of one night spent with him.

I study him, wondering again if I should bring up the kiss. Or if I should just lean in and kiss him myself. I allow myself to imagine what his hands might feel like sliding up my legs right now, pushing past the edge of my robe. Maybe following the same path Coz's hands took last night. My pulse picks up speed at the thought of it.

Owen's face cracks into a smile—almost like he's throwing in the "double dog" part of the dare as he cocks his head to one side, daring me to confirm that matching him with a client would require us to spend just one intimate night together. I'm feeling bold enough to not back down from his little dare this time.

"That *is* how my business works," I say, setting my glass down on the table and meeting the challenging look in his eyes with one of my own. I slide my knees open just a fraction of an inch, with his palms still resting on top of them. The heat from his hands seeps deeper into my bare skin.

My entire body is screaming for him to touch me in other places, too. *Just do it, Owen.* Just this once.

Any other day, Owen would laugh and tell me that he's not sure if he will ever be ready for a serious relationship or match. But there's something about being here together, on this yacht. Because today he's actually placing himself in the position of being matched. And everything that goes along with my matchmaking services.

I can't help but egg him on as his gaze stays locked on mine, neither of us willing to look away yet. The challenge hanging in the air between us is so thick I can almost taste it. I shift in my chair when I recognize how much I want him to throw me on my bed right this second. Praying my face isn't betraying me, I imagine what the first agonizing moments of his mouth on mine might feel like before he ripped my robe off—me pulling desperately at the buttons on his shirt—right before we gave in to over a decade of this rising tension built up between us.

But Owen blinks first and leans back against his chair again, the moment slowly deflating and passing us by as quickly as it had sprung up. I sigh, probably too loud, and sit back in my chair too, trying to slow my breath and pulse back down to a normal rate again.

Thankfully, Owen speaks first.

"I saw you drinking a Coors Light with lime last night," he finally says. I curl one leg up under my body, quickly closing the opening of my robe back over my legs. When I look up again, he's shifting his gaze away from me.

"It sounded good to me." I shrug, forcing myself to take another sip of my juice as nonchalantly as I can, but my body just keeps frolicking inside like we're gearing up for a fuck. I try not to conjure up the taste of the beer from last night—or the look Owen gave me when he saw me nursing the bottle.

"I used to drink those back in college," he says, his eyes searching mine again.

"I know," I say, acting unbothered. Then I can't stop my-self—I meet his eyes, smiling from under my lashes. "I remember."

He laughs now and shakes his head at me, rolling his fin-gers through his hair as he stares back up at the ceiling. This man is more than I can take sometimes. I have been tangled up in his charm for years, and if matching him with a client meant that we would get to share a night—just one night together— maybe it would be worth it. Even if I had to hand him off to someone else in the end.

There has always been a part of me that suspected Owen could be my everything—my person, my lover, my forever. Not just my chosen family like he is now. A bigger part suspects that if we were to try being in a relationship and things went south,

I'd lose him forever. I've always told myself that if he wanted more, he'd have made a move by now. That's the voice in my head that I keep listening to. But at the same time, we've never gone this far down the matchmaker rabbit hole, and the suspense is killing me.

"So you didn't really answer my question," I say, turning the conversation back to hooking him up with a client. I probably shouldn't push it, but he's never let the conversation go this far down that road of possibilities before. Something in me is screaming to change the subject. To take it back, to keep this door closed. But I don't. I don't know what's gotten into me this week—the Coors Light, the moment with the dress on the balcony—now this. Whatever *this* is. "Are you telling me you're ready to be matched? Even if it means spending the night together?"

No sooner are the words out of my mouth that I wish I could crouch down on the floor and hide under the bed from whatever answer he gives me. Because no matter what he says, it won't be what I want to hear. I'm not sure if I want to know whether Owen's ready for a real relationship, especially if it's not with me. And truthfully, I'm not sure if I'm ready for one either. I haven't dated anyone since I lost my fiancé. Not in any real way.

When he doesn't answer me immediately, my heart starts pulling inside like it's beginning to unravel. I wish I could take it back. Just as I'm about to let him off the hook, he speaks.

"No, babe," he says to me, his voice gravelly. "In all seriousness, I'm not sure I'll ever be ready for you to match me with someone." It feels like a rejection. Like I'm twenty years old and I've just tried to kiss him before he lets me down easy again.

I turn away before he can see disappointment seep into my face.

"Lifelong bachelor, Owen Hawking, dies alone in his bed at the age of eighty-two. Half-eaten by his cat before anyone found him …" I ramble on in my best sullen newscaster voice, staring out at the sea.

"Totally unrealistic." He laughs. "I don't even have a cat."

"You've made your bed," I say, turning up my nose and taking a hard bite of my banana while maintaining eye contact.

He finishes laughing before collecting himself and continuing. "Okay then. And what about you, Miss Newscaster? You're not exactly rushing into a relationship. Not even remotely." I know he's just challenging me again.

I'm done with this conversation. "I'm pretty sure that part of me is broken." I huff. The pain of Owen's rejection mingles with the reminder that, at the end of the day, I'm very much alone. And possibly broken inside from a certain level of loss no one should ever have to endure. I may very well be alone forever. It's almost too much to think about.

"I know," he begins quietly. "You lost a lot. It was pretty awful. And then …" He trails off. "When it was over, I thought I might lose you, too. I've never been as scared as I was when I watched what you went through. While I just—" He nearly chokes on the words and I can't take my eyes off him.

He leans in and spins my chair toward him so we're just inches apart. He firmly takes my face between his hands and holds me there, forcing me to face him. "You need to listen to me," he starts again.

A tear trickles down my face before he gently wipes his thumb across my cheek to catch it without letting me go. "I know what happened broke you. But you're *not* broken." His eyes fill with his own tears and memories of the months following the accident. We so rarely discuss the horror of what I went through. He clears his throat, not letting any tears fall, and continues. "But you did survive it. You're still here. And you're the strongest person I know." He pauses, searching my eyes softly now. "If you want to be with somebody … you should be."

The words I want to say are right on the tip of my tongue: *Just not you?* Instead, I stare back at him, aching for him to kiss me.

He slowly adds, "Have you ever thought about … you know, giving a romantic relationship another try?" He's staring at me so hard, I wonder if he can hear my heart beating out of my chest.

"I don't think so," I whisper back. And it's the truth. Most days, I'm a blond bombshell dripping with confidence, wheeling and dealing with the rich and famous. But every now and then, a conversation like this reminds me that there's still a lot of broken glass inside my heart.

He releases my face and sits back with a sigh.

"You're as stubborn as you are strong," he says, looking defeated.

"But that's just the thing, Owen. Sometimes I don't *want* to be strong. All I want is to lose myself in whatever arms are holding me for the night. Then I pick my clothes up off the floor, say an easy goodbye, and pass them off to my happy client. We all win. Nobody gets hurt. No risk to—" The last word catches in my throat and I let my eyes bore into him fully now, more resolute than ever. "This is just who I am. I can't help it if this isn't what you want for me."

There's pain behind his eyes while he watches me dig my heels in. Flustered, I grab a strawberry from the tray and sit back again, suddenly exhausted. I did not come here to pick at the scar tissue on my heart. I came here to celebrate, to meet new matches, and to enjoy my best friend—in the only way I can.

Owen takes a long, steadying breath before speaking again. "I wasn't trying to push. It's just that you deserve the world." He puts his hand over mine and sighs. "I hope you'll feel ready for the real thing again one day. And when you are …"

I take my hand out from under his.

Then I stubbornly look at him, both of us apologizing through the silence that hangs between us: For who we are, and for who we can't be. As much as I would love a romantic future with him or anyone else, the idea feels impossible.

"You deserve the world too," I say, squeezing his hand again. Then I give him a weak smile. "The thought of you being half-eaten by your imaginary cat when you die alone in your bed one day is pretty dark …"

My lips purse together as I tilt my head to the side. He manages to laugh at this, and folds himself back into his chair, grabbing his glass off the table again. He looks as defeated as I feel. I love the way his nose shows its slight, adorably crooked dip when he laughs like that. With all the billions of dollars he has in the bank, he's never attempted to fix it from the surfing injury he got sophomore year. Another thing I love about him.

He squeezes my knee one more time before sliding his hand away, but my heart swells a little less this time. We sit for a few minutes in silence, both of us lost in thought as we stare out the balcony doors.

"So," he says, breaking the silence before taking another sip, "Zara is officially matched with Coz now?" His turn to change the subject, I guess. "Do you get the sense that Channing might be a good fit for Audra after meeting him?"

The weight of what lies ahead of me this week hits me like a tidal wave again, but shop talk is familiar ground and I feel more steady diving into this topic than I did a moment ago.

"Whoever I end up matching with Audra has to be willing to share," I remind him. "She's looking for a guy who doesn't mind bringing another man back into bed with them."

"So that's going to be part of his audition then? Sleeping with Channing and another guy?"

"I really do have the best job," I reply, grinning sideways at him, but there's less gusto behind my voice this time.

"Well shit, if you can't find anyone else to be that third wheel, I can always have Liz check my availability," he says, then laughs. I can tell he's kidding. At least, after that doozy of a conversation, I think he's kidding.

"I'm not so sure you're the sharing type," I say, following his lead into this imaginary scenario. For one quick second, I allow myself to imagine spending a night with both Channing *and* Owen at the same time. One wrapped around me up top while another hits hard from below. *Oh my God.*

"I know how to share," he says, lifting his eyes to mine.

Just then, there's a firm knock on the door. I assume it's a staffer, so I call out, "It's open!"

The door clicks open, but to my surprise, it's not a polo-clad staff member.

It's Coz.

14

"Morning, Cher, Owen." Coz greets us both warmly then strides toward the table with our uneaten breakfast still strewn out around it. His sizable cowboy boots have made their way back onto his feet.

"Uh, good morning," I say, giving Owen a sideways glance that screams *really*? Owen knows that my potential matches sometimes get confused about who they belong to after we've spent a night together, but it's pretty rare.

"I must have missed my invitation to breakfast," Coz says good-naturedly, gesturing to the spread before us. His eyes are shifting around like he's either nervous or slightly annoyed that Owen is here. He clears his throat again awkwardly as we stare at him, waiting for an explanation.

"Help yourself," I say casually, eyeing Owen again. "Can I help you with something?"

"I just came to see how you're doing this morning. I had a great time last night." He looks at me, then Owen, and back at me. Owen must sense my hesitation about the dominance Coz is clearly trying to project because he isn't showing any sign of leaving us alone. I'm grateful for that, even though it's making everything ten times more awkward right now.

"I had a great time too. You did great," I say, but my smile stops just short of reaching my eyes. "And I've already let Zara know that you two are an official match. She's thrilled." I pause to smile, all the way up to my eyes this time. "My assistant Daisy will be calling you later this morning about the date we're setting up for you two. Sometime after we get back to the States."

I pause pointedly. I should probably have Daisy start working up their date details sooner rather than later. It'll be something Coz can focus on, instead of me.

"We'll be in touch," I say firmly. Then I get up from the table. "But I need to start getting ready for the day now. You're welcome to take any of this back to your room." I wave my hands around the tray of food we've hardly touched. Between the horrific flashback this morning and my confusing chat with Owen, I've officially lost my appetite.

"That's it then, huh?" Coz suddenly looks a little annoyed, then turns to Owen. "I don't know how you've managed to hang on to this one so long, my friend. A bit prickly in the morning, isn't she?"

I stand and turn my back to Coz, pretending to look for my phone so he can't see my face turn red from anger. He's a persistent bugger, but I'm wrolling to let it slide because other-wise, I think he's a great match for Zara. He's probably just a bit flustered and attached after last night. Thankfully Owen steps in. He rises from the table and pats Coz on the back, giving him a big smile while steering the lumbering oil tycoon toward the door with him.

"Let's go down to the dining room and see who else is up at this ungodly hour," Owen says as he maneuvers Coz out the door. "We'll see you back on deck later, Cher!" Owen calls back to me without breaking his stride. He throws me a sideways glance before mouthing *you've got this* over his shoulder at me.

Before they disappear into the hallway, Owen flips the lock on my door.

Owen knows Coz is harmless, if not a little too persistent in dragging out his audition, especially after what we shared last night. I hope Coz's misplaced attachment doesn't cause any more problems for me the rest of this week. I need to feel things out with Channing without any more interruptions or distractions.

My phone pings in my hand. It's a text from Audra:

I love you, Cher, but I'm not happy. It's been almost four months. Your contract will be void by the end of the week if you can't deliver. If Channing isn't the right fit, I'm moving on.

I groan and fight the urge to throw my phone off the balcony. Instead, I text her back:

Understood. He's an incredible catch. Definite interest. Will keep you posted on the match. Chat soon.

I slip my phone into my robe pocket and beeline straight toward my dressing room. It's not exactly a lie. Interest *is* there —I just can't tell if it's coming from him yet, or just me.

Pushing aside dresses and jumpsuits, I snatch a pink Chanel minidress off the rack and hold it up to my body. Not too formal, but flashy enough that it will draw plenty of attention. Hopefully from Channing, in particular. Next, I grab a gold Versace bikini with a row of delicate gold chains connecting the thin triangles of fabric just as I hear my phone ping again.

You have until the end of the week.

I sigh and throw my phone onto the plush velvet rug at my feet and sink onto the floor.

I have four days to become better acquainted with Channing, get him interested in Audra, and complete his Full 360 Audition—*with* another man in the bed.

I cover my face with my hands as my stomach starts spiraling toward the floor. When Channing's impossibly gorgeous face pops into my head, I can't help but smile.

If I can pull this whole thing off, it's going to be so worth it.

15

I pop a grape into my mouth and scan the deck. "You're gonna sit right here. Even if it takes all day," I mumble to myself.

I've been sitting here for nearly an hour, soaking up the sun and trying to spot Channing, but I haven't seen him any-where yet.

A large group of guests took sixteen of the ship's jet skis out to hit the waves earlier this afternoon, and I can see them all flying around the harbor like a gang of ragdolls hanging on for dear life. Just the sight of it makes me dizzy, and I nudge my plate aside.

Closer to shore is another group of guests Owen had fer-ried out to catch the surf this morning. Owen surfs back home in Malibu like it's his religion, but knowing he's out there right now bobbing on the surface of those waves pinches at the edge of my nerves. I need to find another place to sit with less of a view. I grab the rim of my plate and get ready to stand when I hear a woman's voice behind me.

"Cher? Cher Thatcher?"

I turn to see Cadence Fisher walking in my direction. A scarlet red Pamella Roland caftan is draped across her porcelain skin as she settles in next to me at the table with a tiny plate of fruit from the lunch service the crew set out earlier. She's wearing an extra-wide brimmed hat with round rose gold Gucci sunglasses perched across the bridge of her tiny nose. She looks like the caricature of a glamorous movie star. It's easy to see how she has one of the world's most recognizable faces.

"I'm sorry, we've never met. You're Owen's friend, Cher, right?"

"Yes. That's me!" I smile warmly, then turn my back to the water, grateful for the distraction even if it is Owen's crush. "You must be Cadence."

She smiles back at me and, against my better wishes, I decide I like her immediately. There's something easy and open about her. She embodies the same natural charisma that most of Owen's social and business circles have. I've come to see it as a mark of the truly successful—the ability to charm the pants off anyone.

"I saw you come in off the helicopter last night," I say. "And I thought I recognized someone else with you … was that Charlie Beckett?" I give her a side-eye and a grin, inviting in the intimacy of a potential newfound friend.

"Yeah, he's out on the jet skis this afternoon. I told him that he'd better come back in one piece." She holds up one hand to shield her eyes as she searches the group of jet skiers for him. We pause to watch as one of them hits a huge wave and gets knocked off it, then resurfaces with a laugh as the jet ski circles them in the water before they can manage to climb back on. Like the surfers, they're all too far out from the ship to recognize anyone in particular so she turns her attention back to me. "A little bird told me you're quite the matchmaker."

I chuckle as she lifts her sunglasses to give me a wide-eyed grin. Once again, my reputation precedes me. The adrenaline rush of owning my hard-earned gravitas hasn't quite worn off yet. I hope it never does.

"I am," I confirm. "The one and only. Why? Isn't Charlie holding your attention this week?" I'm prying a bit, but she did bring up the subject of matching. Plus, I'm curious whether Cadence and Charlie are here together, for Owen's sake.

"Charlie and me?" She laughs and swats at the air between us. "Oh God, no. Charlie's chopper pilot got sick at the last minute yesterday, and we happened to be taking off from the same private airport back on shore. I told him he could bum a ride in with me."

She leans in intimately. "He's handsome as hell, but way too charming for his own good. In case you're wondering, the tabloids haven't gotten anything wrong about him. That man probably isn't even loyal to his own mother." Then she tips back her head and laughs, grabbing my hand.

I breathe a sigh of relief, which instantly morphs into envy. Owen will be happy to know that Cadence didn't come with Charlie as her date this week, after all. My smile fades for just a moment before I can shake it off.

"So the rumors are true then? Charlie is a bit of a playboy?" I ask, hoping she'll keep talking so I don't have to.

"Of course. I'd always heard he was a horny little monkey, but when he confessed his love for me, like, twenty minutes into our flight and then asked me to join the mile-high club with him ..."

I nearly snort before bursting into a full laugh, trying to picture how that would work. "How does one join the mile-high club in a helicopter?" I ask.

"I had the same question!" She's laughing now too. "He told me that the pilot wouldn't mind. And that we could get creative." She raises her eyebrows at me with a funny frown. Cadence is impossible to look away from. Between her natural beauty and loads of charisma, I can see how she's caught Owen's eye. She continues like we're old friends already. "Obviously I told the ol' horn dog to get lost. When he finally stopped pestering me, we spent the rest of the flight playing Fuck, Marry, Kill with Owen's guest list."

I laugh again. She's beautiful *and* funny. She'll have Owen wrapped around her long, manicured finger in no time.

"You mile-high heartbreaker, you" I manage. "Back up though. What game did you play?"

"Oh my god, stop!" she shrieks, grabbing my arm. "You've never played Fuck, Marry, Kill?"

"I've never played," I say seriously, spearing a raspberry.

She explains that whoever you're playing with gives you three names and you have to choose which of the three you'd choose to marry, which one you'd sleep with, and which one you'd kill.

"Your name came up on Charlie's *fuck list*," she adds coyly.

"Great," I laugh, taking a dramatic swig of my Bloody Mary. "I didn't realize Charlie Beckett knew my name."

"Oh, honey, he knows more than your name. You're as famous as he is in our circles. I think you have the best job," she says dreamily, nudging my elbow.

I smile back at her. She's not wrong.

"Not to mention you're absolutely stunning," she continues, biting into a deep red cherry that matches her lips. "He couldn't stop talking about your last set of photos in the tabloids."

I laugh. "I didn't realize Charlie Beckett wasted his time with trashy magazines."

"Oh Lord, yes, he's a total media whore," she says. "On the way over, he showed me that gaudy article the *Weekly* did about all the bigwigs coming out here this weekend. It featured that paparazzi shot of you and Owen from the last time you two were in Saint-Tropez together." She pops another cherry into her mouth, but I notice her vibe has switched from lighthearted to a tad bit more serious. "What is it with you and Owen anyway? Are you two an item?"

I can tell from the way she's looking at me intently that this is the real reason she came to sit down next to me. She wants to know whether I'm a threat when it comes to her and Owen's budding romance. I can respect that. And as much as I'd love to sabotage this situation, I don't.

"Owen and I go way back as friends. I'm just with him a lot of the time when the paparazzi shows up for those shots, so I get photographed too," I explain.

"So you're single like me." She smiles brightly again. "So … who is Owen seeing these days if it's not you?" she asks, this time squinting at me through her sunglasses.

I'm grateful she moves on so quickly. The number of times I have to reassure someone that there is no romantic link between Owen and me is a little ridiculous. Just once I'd like to tell someone that we secretly fuck every night of the week, and mean it. "I don't think he's seeing anyone right now," I say with just a touch of wistfulness.

She perks up at this and looks at me suspiciously. "How is that even possible? He's so unbelievably hot. And loaded."

"Why?" I ask. "Are you in the market for a match? Because I think I know a guy." I smile at her, unsure of what else to say at this point.

"I might be," she says mischievously. "But I'm not sure I need matchmaking services. I think I might try the old-fashioned way first."

"With Owen?" I confirm. Owen hasn't gotten involved in anything serious the whole time we've known each other, preferring to play along the edges of romance with mostly physical connections and brief flings over the years. The tabloids are constantly going on about how he's the world's most eligible bachelor. Still, he did seem more excited about a potential connection with Cadence this week. And now I can see why. She's easy to talk to, and even as a straight woman, I can't seem to keep my eyes off her. The way she moves and makes effortless conversation is mesmerizing.

"Sorry to bring it up again, but I have to ask. You've never taken the plunge with him," she confirms, leaning in intimately. "So, woman-to-woman, what's wrong with him?"

I pop a cube of mango in my mouth and bite down hard, giving myself a moment to think. *How do I put this?* There's no way I'm digging up all the broken glass in my heart again with her right now.

"Owen is the best man I know," I say finally. Her eyes widen and I can tell she's touched by my honesty as much as my answer.

"Then why …"

"Because it's *Owen*. He's been my best friend since I was eighteen. He's my family at this point. Nothing is more important than that."

"And that's your only reason?" She eyes me again. "He's like a brother to you?"

"Better than a brother," I tell her truthfully. "Owen is incredible. Whether it's you or someone else, he will make whoever he falls in love with unbelievably happy one day."

She's still watching me carefully, so I continue. My heart is breaking a little in talking him up to someone else, but I don't want to be the reason he misses out on this beautiful woman.

So I keep going. "He pays attention to the smallest details when it's anything he cares about—whether it's his work or the people he loves. You'd be shocked to hear how many times he's read my mind or knows exactly what I want or need without me ever having to say a word. He just knows because he pays attention. And he's funny. Like *really* funny. He can make the most mundane moments memorable. Then there's his ambition. You'll never meet another man as ambitious as Owen. He's—"

I force myself to stop rambling. My heart is pounding. I suddenly want to end this conversation as fast as I can.

Thankfully, Cadence jumps in. "He *does* sound better than a brother." She laughs. "But you *do* sound like you might like— or love him." All jokes aside, she's suddenly studying me like a hawk.

"I do," I say, and I mean it with my whole heart. "Just not the way you think." That's a lie, but I can see that she buys it.

She watches me for a moment and then slowly rests her hand on my arm.

"You were engaged once before, right?" she says softly and I nod. "I remember reading something about that boating accident in the tabloids. I'm so sorry." There's genuine sympathy in her eyes, but I look away, not wanting to play the victim.

"I'm happy where I'm at in my life now." I manage to smile at her, then shift the subject back to her. "Just let me know if you ever want me to play matchmaker for you."

"I'm not sure I could stomach the idea of you fully auditioning Owen then passing him on to me," she says with a weak smile and I appreciate the honesty. I'm not sure I could handle the part where I pass Owen off to her either. "Not because I don't like your business. I think it's amazing. And honestly, empowering. But …" She trails off, looking out at the water.

"You don't need my help," I reassure her. "And neither does Owen. You're both incredible, and you have this whole week to figure things out with each other."

I know Owen will be ready to settle down one day when he falls in love. And when he does, I'll have to take a backseat to whoever he brings into his life. In fact, I'll have to welcome whoever it is like family if I plan to keep him as my family too. That woman could end up being Cadence.

"Thanks for the chat, Cher." She pats my hand, looking out at the waves for Charlie or Owen before picking up her mimosa and swirling the liquid around. A gust of wind picks up as we hear the ship's sleek black chopper making its way to the helipad again. "I bet that's the first group coming back from shore." Cadence grabs the edges of her hat so it doesn't fly away in the sudden bluster from the chopper.

The runners are just touching down when I look over the railing to see who's landing on the helipad. The door opens and Channing jumps out with his wetsuit unzipped down past his hips.

His tan skin is slick with beads of water droplets glistening in the sun. He pushes his dark hair back with a free hand. I don't even notice who gets out behind him—I'm too focused on the way his muscles ripple across his back as he jogs to the edge of the helipad. He has an intense look about him that I can't take my eyes off of. Before I can stop myself, I imagine what type of intensity he'd bring into the bedroom with a look like that.

I'm practically drooling by the time I turn back to Cadence and see that she's been wistfully watching Channing, too.

We make eye contact and giggle, realizing we've both been transfixed by the ship's best view of the day.

"Hot damn, that one is a whole snack," she exhales breathlessly. "I've heard he can be quite the lion in bed, too. Maybe too serious for me though. Not really my type. But that doesn't mean I can't enjoy the way he looks soaking wet and half naked." She laughs.

Any woman with a pulse would appreciate the way Channing Stanbury looks in a wetsuit—still salty and dripping from the surf. He's probably going to his room now to get ready for the night ahead. I wish I could trail behind him to get our audition underway when that wetsuit comes off.

I give Cadence a quick hug and excuse myself from the table so I can get myself ready for the night ahead as well.

Owen's team has invited everyone to a costumed Fallen Angels masquerade-themed party tonight on deck. I've chosen a dark, devilish look for the heaven-and-hell theme. The crew is already starting to transform the deck into an ethereal landscape to match the party. I need to start my transformation too.

Stealing one last glance at Channing, I watch as he rinses himself off under one of the ship's outdoor showers, his wetsuit still hanging loosely around his hips. I admire the way his abs dip into the top of a V, just above the neoprene edge of fabric. Before I can help it, I imagine what he'd look like if that wetsuit were to slide just a little lower. Maybe all the way off.

I hope I'm lucky enough to find out.

16

Four hours later, after washing, waxing, primping, and practically getting sewn into my costume, I'm ready to party.

My glam team nailed my Fallen Angel look, placing hundreds of black Swarovski crystals across my cheekbones into a stunning half-mask that accentuates the smokey charcoal eye makeup they did to complete the look. The black Leavers lace jumpsuit hugging every curve I have is the real show stopper tonight. Leavers handcrafted the lace to fit me like a glove a few months ago while on a shopping expedition in northern France, and it was worth every euro. The delicate material feels as exquisite as it looks.

If I can't catch Channing's eye in this, then he might not have a working pulse.

Owen nearly fell over earlier tonight when he came to my room and saw this sheer lace outfit before the party started. He clutched his heart and took a step back when I came out of the dressing room to see him standing next to my bed in a classic tux and black mask with two flutes of Crystal for us. It took everything in me not to tackle him onto the sheets right then and there. He looked and smelled so good.

As I strut onto the party deck, I see that the *MaryLou* crew has fully transformed the ship into a glowing red hellscape. Deep scarlet lights cover the ship in a sexy, mysterious mood. A few deckhands rush past me to secure a tarp that has started to flap in the wind. I notice the warm breeze from this afternoon seems to have picked up since leaving the deck behind earlier.

You're fine, I remind myself. This yacht is enormous. A little wind isn't going to hurt us.

After scanning the crowd for Owen or Channing—no luck spotting either of them yet—I'm happy to see that everyone on deck has taken the costume assignment as seriously as me. A few Victoria's Secret runway models must have smuggled their enormous wings onboard. Owen is laughing with one of them as they clink tiny crystal shot glasses together and throw them back without so much as a wince. The woman standing at his arm must be six-foot-three in her sexy lace-up stilettos, with her wings splayed out even higher than that behind her. The whole effect is like a stunning work of art.

Another incredible Grammy-winning artist is onstage now belting out one of her biggest hits while a lively swarm of cos-tumed party-goers are already tearing up the dance floor.

I somehow managed to tell Owen about my conversation with Cadence earlier in the day. He seemed genuinely excited about her interest in him, and the fact that Charlie isn't in the picture romantically. Sometimes I feel like I deserve a gold medal for friendship when it comes to setting my romantic feelings aside when it's something I know will make Owen happy.

Another gust of wind whips up around me from an incoming chopper, but when I glance at the helipad to see who's arriving, I'm startled to see there's no helicopter coming in or out. It's just the wind. The gusts are coming in harder, which means I'm going to need a strong distraction from it to settle my nerves.

I bump my way through the crowd to order a drink from the nearest bar and break into a smile. "French 95, please. Double twist," I say, saddling up to the counter where the sexy Australian bartender from the night before is standing.

"No Coors Light tonight?" He leans in, holding his weight against the bartop with both hands to give me his full attention. The tips must be good if he makes every woman onboard feel like this with his undivided attention.

The Saint-Tropez sun has gifted him with a deeper tan than he had last night—popping against his gorgeous pale green eyes and thick black lashes.

He rolls up his sleeves and I glance at the tattoos layered across the muscles in his forearms. I'm attracted to every visible inch of him. And I'm sure, if given the chance, that attraction would carry over to every non-visible inch too. I silently thank Owen for hiring this feast of a man to craft cocktails aboard the *MaryLou* this week.

"Not tonight," I reply. "I decided to up my game with something a bit more classier." If Channing would just get his fine ass out here tonight, this guy might be the perfect no-strings addition to his audition.

"Classy suits you," the bartender says in that rugged Australian accent. He gets to work on the cocktail but brazenly lets his eyes wander down my jumpsuit with appreciation. He clearly doesn't mind if I see him looking down at my curves. Normally I wouldn't seek out this kind of blatant attention from a stranger, but something about our natural chemistry makes his wandering eyes a turn-on. And this lace jumpsuit is making me feel extra sexy tonight.

"Having any fun out here?" I ask.

"A bit of fun here and there." He grins cheekily and his dimples deepen. I can tell he's caught my subtle meaning by the slightest pink that rolls across his cheeks. "But not necessarily with everyone I'd want a bit of fun with." He pauses. "Yet."

I laugh. Now it's my turn to blush. He could be a model with those cheekbones.

He goes on. "Normally I wouldn't pry—"

"No?" I interrupt him. "You don't seem like the type that wouldn't pry." We both laugh. Our banter is on point and I like that I'm keeping him on his toes.

"In my line of work," he continues through a smile, "I thought I'd seen it all by now. So I'm pretty curious. What was the situation with that big guy the other night? That whole '*for Zara*' thing?"

I take a sip of the drink he's given me. Champagne bubbles and bourbon dance across the tip of my tongue, finishing with the intoxicating scent of a double lemon twist. A single orange blossom floats alongside a fresh sprig of rosemary. Everything about his concoction is beautiful.

"This drink is amazing," I tell him. "Where did you learn to bartend?"

"Nice try," he says, and I laugh. "You don't have to tell me, if you don't want to." I appreciate that he's giving me an out, but I don't take it. I'd rather go fishing for a third wheel.

"I'm a matchmaker," I say proudly. "I find women the love of their life. I was auditioning a match for my client, Zara, last night."

"By taking that guy back to his room?"

"Yes," I confirm boldly. I wasn't always so confident about telling people what I do, or how my business works. His thick brows furl together in confusion, so I go on. "My clients are some of the most beautiful and successful women in the world. They don't have time to date around. When they do have time, they don't want to waste it on someone who isn't going to make them *completely* happy."

I pause and look at him pointedly.

"Oh. You, er, you—" He's grasping for the polite way to say it. But I kind of enjoy watching him struggle a bit, so I don't fill it in for him right away. I smile and blink back at him, seeing what he can come up with. Finally he stammers, "You—um— you test the *men* for them?"

Another guest to my right orders a gin and tonic. He twists open a bottle of Nolet's Reserve and gets to work but keeps his eyes glued on me, continuing our conversation.

"Well, yeah, but I test everything else for them first. That's just the last step. If a potential match makes it through every other part of the audition process, then I make sure my client will be happy with them in the bedroom. If that's what they want." I wait for a strong reaction from him, but there isn't one. He's simply listening without judgment. Maybe he truly has seen it all.

"That's actually brilliant." He stares at me, genuinely impressed. A petite little devil with a feather boa draped across each shoulder comes up to the counter and asks for a round of Patrón. The Aussie starts preparing the tequila shots as he continues. "And you really make a good living doing this?"

"I get by," I say, laughing. He clearly hasn't read the tabloids.

"Fascinating," he breathes out in awe. Then he hands the small silver tray of shots to the little devil. She turns around to take them back to her group of girlfriends with a high-pitched whistle. "You wouldn't happen to have any clients looking for a half-decent bartender who can make a killer French 95, would you?" He's teasing, but it opens the door for what I've been thinking of asking him.

"Actually, I *do* have one client looking for someone who's looking for something French," I say.

When he raises his eyebrows, I add, "A ménage à trois."

I watch him closely, knowing his immediate reaction will tell me everything I need to know. Surprisingly, he looks pretty relaxed about it.

"Boy, did I go into the wrong profession." He laughs, shaking his head happily. He takes a cloth to wipe up a spot of water.

I press a little more. "The guy I'm trying to match her with is here this week. If everything goes well, I'll need to bring another man in to see how he handles sharing in bed. On behalf of my client, of course."

"Who's the potential match?"

I look behind me to scan the crowd for Channing. *Bingo.* He's finally here. I turn back to the bartender and raise my eyebrows when I finally spot Channing. "You've probably seen him around. He's the one in the tux with the black Zorro-looking mask over there."

He chuckles again. "That doesn't really narrow it down, but I think I can see who you're pointing out."

There's a sea of men in black tuxes with similar masks. I spot one of the Amazonian Victoria's Secret angels trying to cozy up to Channing. She's rubbing her hand up his chest, and he's not acting the least bit upset about it. The model's friend, another Victoria's Secret angel, cozies up to him on the other side. *Wonderful.*

Time to quit wasting my time here and make a connection with Channing before it's too late and he ends the night getting worshipped by those two angels.

"So you're game?" I quickly ask.

He nods back at me, smiling. "Is that even a question?"

"Then I'll find you later if I need you!" I turn to go. "Wait, what's your name?" I ask, spinning back around.

"Aaron—" He nearly gets his last name out, but I interrupt him. No time to waste.

"Okay, Aaron, I'll let you know if I—if we—if—" I'm not sure how to phrase it, so I just smile and cock my head at him.

"Of course," he says, laughing. Then he writes his number on the back of a card and slips it into my hand. "Go get 'em, gorgeous." Oh lord, that accent. He's going to make a fun addition later if I can just get Channing to agree to this whole thing.

I turn and make my way through the bouncing crowd toward my mark.

17

Before I can reach Channing, Coz blocks my path.

"Well hello there, little lady." His size makes it impossible for me to see my actual target behind him.

"Hi, Coz," I say, trying to hide how annoyed I am.

"That outfit is—" He whistles instead of finishing the sentence. I interrupt him before he can get another word out.

"Thank you! You look handsome too." Then I push past him. It's like a fantasy land of costumed models and actresses out here. I need to land my match for Audra tonight, and quickly, considering how hot all the guests on deck look.

"See you later!" Coz yells over the music at me as I walk past a speaker. I ignore him but look over my shoulder to make sure he's staying put instead of following me through the crowd. Then I head into the mass of guests on the dance floor to get to Channing.

Midway through the crowded dance floor, I spot Cadence dancing with Owen, lost in their own world. She reaches up to touch his cheek as they share an intimate laugh together, nearly touching foreheads. Without watching where I'm going, I bump

into the back of somebody just as a shoe lands on my foot—
sending searing pain through my toe. Wincing, I lift up my foot
to rub it while trying to balance on my other heel in the rowdy
crowd.

"Excuse me," I say with an edge to my voice, even though
it was me who wasn't looking where I was going.

I look up from my foot to see who has just stepped on me.
It's Channing.

Suddenly, I'm flung into him again as a dancer to my left
bumps me hard.

"Cher!" he exclaims. He looks as surprised as I am. "Did I
hurt you? I'm so sorry," he shouts over the thumping music.

"Channing," I breathe out his name, then look down at my
pulsing toe. "I'm fine," I shout back, but I grab onto his bicep
with one hand to balance myself on my stiletto while I hold my
injured foot with the other. His muscle feels like a granite boul-
der under my hand.

I try putting my foot back on the ground, but cringe and
lift it back up again. I can't let a little toe injury ruin my opportunity to talk to him, but I can't put any weight on it yet. We're
bumped again from the other side, and Channing wraps an arm
around my waist to keep me from falling.

We're getting jostled and pushed together by the crowd
around us as the musician continues belting out one of her biggest crowd-pleasers. Someone knocks me from behind yet again.
Channing steadies me so I can take the weight off my foot. The
pain eases immediately when I realize that his muscular hands
are resting just above my hips. I lean into him so I don't fall

when another pair of dancing guests jostle into me from behind. Every time I try to bend down to look at the damage to my foot, I nearly tip over.

"Let's get you off the dance floor," he says.

"I'm sure I'll be fine!" I call over the music into his ear. I'm not fine, but this is not the entrance I wanted to make.

"Follow me," he says, leaning near my ear so I can hear him over the music. He smells amazing. Like ocean air, clean bedsheets, and spicy pine needles all shaken up together in a bottle. "I want to get a closer look at that foot."

I don't argue. This is my opportunity to have Channing all to myself so I let him slide his arm around my rib cage and pull me tightly against him. One of his hands plants firmly where my bra band would be—if I was wearing one.

After pushing our way through the crowd, he guides me to a tall cocktail table standing in a much quieter corner of the deck. I try to hoist myself up onto the table-height chair, but I'm struggling with just one foot.

"May I?" he asks.

Without waiting for my reply, he spins me around and picks me up by the hips to sit me down on the seat. It's effortless. Like I'm nothing more than a delicate doll to him.

I start to lift my foot to examine it, but he crouches beside me and runs his hands down my calf, cupping his palm ever so gently around my heel to lift it. I can't take my eyes off him. The intensity of his expression as he studies my exposed skin is making me melt.

He gently maneuvers my toes back and forth in the dim lighting, studying my foot like there will be a test later. There's already a wicked purple bruise forming that extends toward the top of my foot. And even in the dim lighting, I can see that it's starting to swell too.

"We need to get you a bag of ice and elevate this before it gets any worse," he says, more to himself than to me. Then he gently lowers my foot and scoops me back up in his arms. My hands wrap around his neck instinctively as he lifts me off the tall chair.

"It's just a bruise," I protest, but he's already walking me toward a lower set of tables and chairs, even farther from the unfolding party.

"I don't think your toe is broken, but you should keep your foot elevated for a bit," he says as he gently sets me down on one of the chairs he's just carried me to.

"Put this up here," he says, placing my foot on the surface of the table next to me. He removes his tuxedo jacket and balls it up under my ankle so the sharp edge of the table won't dig into my skin.

"You're quite the medic," I say slowly, admiring the way he's naturally driven to take care of me, trying hard not to swoon. *This guy is for Audra*, a voice inside my head reminds me. It's the first time I've had to check myself not to think of a potential match as anything other than a means to a happy ending for my client.

"I actually spent some time in the army as a medic," he says as he adjusts my ankle on the balled up jacket so it's stable. His eyes follow the curve of my leg. "This jumpsuit is unreal."

"Leavers lace from Sakae," I say. "They do incredible work if you're ever in northern France and in the market for a lace jumpsuit." His eyes meet mine and he breaks into a grin.

"I'll keep that in mind," he says with a quiet laugh, and I feel myself flush. "Listen, stay put. I'm going to ask the crew to bring me an ice pack. Don't move a muscle."

I happily obey, and a moment later, he's back with a cold gel pack. He sits next to me and gently holds it up to where my foot is starting to swell. I yelp when it hits my skin.

"Sorry," he says. When our eyes connect, I'm taken aback by the genuine concern etched on his face. It's just a little toe injury, but I may as well be bleeding to death here, judging by the way he's caring for me. Like I'm the most precious thing on earth. "Let me see if I can find something to make this ice a little less … icy for you." He looks around and grabs a cloth napkin off a nearby table, then wraps it around the pack to shield my skin from the cold. "Is that any better?"

When he looks at me for an answer, I struggle to find any words to respond. The way he's watching me right now has my stomach twisted in knots. I look away to distract myself from how hot he looks down there. If I was going off our sexual chemistry alone, I'd be ready to audition him without waiting another second. But I have a bit more digging to do for Audra.

"Yep, that feels a little better. Thanks," I manage to say, meeting his eyes again. Neither of us looks away immediately, but I break eye contact first.

I need to shake this off—whatever it is I'm feeling— for Audra's sake, but for some reason, I can't. I'm wildly attracted to Channing. Animalistically, instinctively, savagely drawn to him. I could pounce on him right here if it meant that I'd never have to let him go. And it's not just how he looks. His appearance is just the icing on the cake. There's something in the air between us that I haven't let myself feel in so long. I don't know what to think about it. I have never felt this way about a potential match for any of my clients. Not once.

"So you spent some time in the army?" I finally manage to form words again, trying to shift the conversation to safe ground. "As a medic? What was that like?"

He pulls the ice back to examine my foot without replying, like he's suddenly lost in thought.

"Well," he starts, then stops again and looks down. He shoots his eyes at me, his lips drawn to one side. "It was—"

"I'm sorry," I rush to say, regretting my question. "You don't have to talk about it if you don't want to. I'm just curious about you." I smile at him appreciatively, then pause again, hoping he'll talk more about himself.

"No, it's not like that," he says. "My time as a combat medic was—it was good. But in an awful way. If that makes sense?" He glances up to search my eyes and I nod at him. I don't want him to stop talking.

He thinks a moment then says, "A lot of what I saw was awful. Obviously." He watches me for a beat before looking back down at my foot and continuing. "But I think it was the best thing I've ever done. Possibly in my whole life. Or, you know, at least the most meaningful thing."

I'm touched by his vulnerability. "I think I know what you mean," I say.

The wind has picked up even more while we've been out here, and the temperature has plummeted. I try my best to ignore it but another chill sweeps through me.

I shiver and rub my hands together.

"You're freezing," he says. "Time for some heat."

He sets the ice down, then pulls my leg off the top of the table, stretching it sideways across his lap. Then he grabs his tuxedo jacket from where it was balled up under my ankle and wraps it around my shoulders instead. It's still warm. "Do you want me to keep rubbing this foot?"

"Is that a serious question?" I ask, laughing with both my brows raised.

"Well, I did just step on you."

I laugh. "I don't mind." And I don't. I'd take bruised toes any day if it meant Channing Stanbury would be touching me like this a little longer.

18

"You know a little about me, but I don't know much about you," Channing says, his intense eyes locking in on mine.

I can tell he wants to change the subject away from him, but my conversations with potential matches are pointedly about them, not about me. I don't want him to stop talking though, and I certainly don't want him to stop rubbing my foot like he is right now.

"Oh you know. I love the typical SoCal girly stuff. Bubble baths, running, and foot massages," I say lightly, smiling down at the foot he's rubbing absentmindedly.

He grins back. "Basic, but nice."

"Did you just call me basic?" I laugh.

"I'll take it back if you tell me something about yourself that's just a little deeper than bubble baths and foot massages," he says, and I laugh again. His eyes crinkle at the sides when he smiles like that, and it makes my stomach feel like it's jumping off a high point. In the best way.

"What do you want to know?" I ask. *Why am I flirting with him?* This conversation should all be about him. Him *and*

Audra. But I can't seem to stop myself. For once, I'm not racing through a running checklist in my head of what another woman wants while I enjoy the company of a gorgeous man. "And you'd better take back what you said about me being basic," I add, smiling.

"I'm sorry." He laughs, shaking his head toward the floor. "I'm usually much smoother than this."

"I think I like this less smooth side of you," I say before silently screaming at myself to stop whatever it is I'm doing, but when he smiles back at me, I know that I'm not going to.

"Tell me about your matchmaking business. Owen mentioned it when we got drinks the other night. After he found out I was single."

"Oh, you're single?" I stifle a grin, trying to feign ignorance.

"Always," he replies.

"What does that mean?" What if he has no interest in an actual relationship? Or even one date with Audra?

"What about you?" he asks, ignoring my question entirely. "Are you single?"

"Always," I repeat, and he slowly breaks into a smile that makes my heart feel like it's melting.

"I find that hard to believe," he says. "How is someone like you not in a relationship?"

A swarm of butterflies flap wildly in my stomach, but it's not just from Channing saying *someone like you*. The ship is rocking more than it has all week as the wind continues to whip up around us. I grip the edges of my chair and fight the urge to run back to my room to hide under the covers. This moment with Channing is what I've been waiting for since I heard he was coming onboard. I can't waste this opportunity over a bit of wind.

"Well," I say, "I'm not your typical matchmaker—"

Just then, the ship hits a strong dip and we're thrown sideways. I shriek and lunge toward him, grabbing his shirt and burying my face in his chest, my knees pushed up in a little ball against him. The ship quickly steadies itself and I release my grip on him, feeling silly for having had such a strong reaction. Breathing heavily, I force myself to lean back from him as he holds my arms in his hands and slowly lowers his face down to mine.

"Whoa, there," he says, running his palms along my arms as if to warm me up, but really I think it's because he can feel my whole body shaking. He takes one hand to lift my chin toward his face. His eyes are dark and stormy, and I hope the sea isn't about to match them. "Just a little dip in the waves, from the wind picking up tonight. It's nothing."

I work to steady my breath as I silently walk myself through some of the calming mantras my counselor's given me over the years.

No flashbacks right now. Please not right now.

19

The *MaryLou* slowly starts pitching to the side more forcefully and I look at Channing, unable to hide my fear. A storm must have rolled in while the party on deck drowned out most of the approaching thunder, but now it's right above us.

"Let's get you inside," he says over the rain after seeing the look on my face. It sounds like the deck is getting pummeled by thousands of tiny golf balls. He lifts me to my feet. My foot is feeling a little better after the ice. Either that, or it's the sudden adrenaline coursing through my veins that's successfully erasing the pain.

"What do we do? What if the ship goes down? We can't get a helicopter to fly us back to shore in this storm," I say, suddenly feeling trapped and panicky. I should have left the ship at the first sign of wind earlier. Now we might be stuck out here and forced to ride it out. I'm trying hard not to lose it, but a bolt of lightning slices across the sky and I jump against him, startled and scared. He can't protect me out here, but I still feel like climbing him like a cat up a tree with nowhere to hide.

He takes my face between his hands as the rain soaks us both.

"Hey … " He's stares straight into my eyes for what feels like an eternity before he goes on. I can tell he has questions about my reaction. It's just wind and waves, but it's so much more than that for me. "It's just a little storm and we're going to be all right," he says. "But I won't leave you alone if you don't want me to. I'm going to take you back to your room so we're not out here when the worst of this storm hits us."

Party guests are shrieking and laughing as they run for cover from the deafening rain. Another lightning bolt strikes the air right above us, and the mood suddenly shifts from lighthearted to more dangerous as the crew starts ushering guests toward hallways and the massive awnings that cover parts of the deck. Another streak of light pierces the black sky all around us followed by a thundering boom that makes me cover my ears. I see Owen's face illuminated for a split second in the light as he wraps one arm around Cadence and they run for cover.

I turn and bury my face in Channing's shoulder as the ship rocks harder—like a little girl hiding under the covers while a monster beckons from beneath the bed.

"Channing," I stutter, unable to move. "I can't—"

"We need to take shelter," he says, sounding calm, but I can tell there's something more urgent in his voice than there was a moment ago.

He throws an arm around my waist again as we quickly make our way back to the crowded hallway that leads to my room.

* * *

When we're safely inside, I immediately shut my curtains to hide the sight of the waves crashing in the shattered moonlight outside the balcony.

The *MaryLou* is still pitching and sliding on the wild ocean as the mounting waves surge higher beneath the ship.

"Would it help you to see what's happening out there?" Channing says gently, pushing the curtains open again.

"No!" I say abruptly, shutting them firmly. "I can't watch."

"Not a fan of the open sea, I take it?" he asks gingerly.

My face must say what I can't.

He nods, then adds, "No offense, but what the hell are you doing out here then?" His quick change in tone makes me laugh, and my panic recedes just a bit.

"No—I mean, I'm fine. It's just ..." I trail off, wanting to change the subject. It's not *fine*. It was never fine. I hate when I use that phrase to make other people feel more comfortable.

"You don't have to say you're fine for my sake," he says.

I look up at him sharply, wondering how much he already knows from the tabloids. He doesn't strike me as much of a trashy magazine reader, but you never know.

His eyes are kind but concerned. He really doesn't know. I'm not sure I'm ready to tell him right now. The silence hangs in the air between us.

"I know that look in your eyes," he says softly. "You already knew my name last night, so you probably know some of my history, too." He pauses. "Or at least what the tabloids have made it out to be."

I nod. He's right. I do know a lot about him from what I've seen run in the tabloids and the news over the years. Like the Vanderbilts and the Rockefellers, Channing's family is American royalty. Extremely wealthy and supremely powerful.

"Then maybe you know that both my parents died when I was sixteen." There's no edge to his voice when he says it, and I'm not sure what to think. I can hardly stand to think about losing my own parents ten years later, but he seems unshaken when he mentions it.

"In a car accident together, right?" I ask quietly. This conversation feels so intimate. I know he's sharing this to help relax my reaction to the storm, but something about his presence puts me at ease. And I let myself lean into it, sitting down on the bed while he sits on the other side.

"Right," he says. "I was your typical teen boy, and then after the accident … well, let's just say I really lost my bearings. My uncle thought the army would straighten me back out." He moves closer to me on the bed.

"And did it?" I ask. In some ways, I already know the answer. Channing has been known in the past for his bad-boy reputation. There are a few photos of him flipping off the cameras when he was much younger, and even a video of him getting after one of the paparazzi who wouldn't leave him alone after a night of clubbing in New York. But, I haven't seen any coverage of him like that in a few years now.

"Not at first, no," he confirms with a guilty smile. "I don't think I started caring about much of anything again until I discovered architectural design and real estate."

This is all making sense. In recent years, Channing has become famous for the unique properties that he designs himself. He's one of the few developers in the world who's more interested in leaving his mark in the aesthetics of a major project than he is in the bottom line. Which he can afford to do with the money he inherited as a young Stanbury heir.

"What were your parents' names?" I ask him gently, needing to know more.

"Talia and Rudy," he says. There's a hint of something deep in his eyes—like he's happy to have someone to remember them with. "Talia and Randolph, actually, but everyone who loved my dad called him Rudy."

"Talia and Rudy," I repeat back.

We watch each other quietly for a beat, soaking in the moment.

Finally, I whisper, "I lost my family … and my fiancé ten years ago."

He studies my face before squeezing my knee lightly. It sends an electric current up my body. "I'm so sorry," he says. It's a simple, but heartfelt answer. I can tell he knows not to overdo the look of pity on his face, or feel the need to say all the right things to me in this moment, which I'm grateful for. He knows what it's like to go through a loss like that, and it seems like we both understand that sometimes just being present with someone when they share something like that can be the best way to respond.

"What were their names?" he asks quietly, reaching for my foot again, alternating a bit between ice and heat.

"My parents were Paul and Sara," I say, my voice trembling like the window rattling from the wind. "My sister's name was Ayla. My fiancé was Trevor."

He repeats their names, and the sound of it sends a current of warmth through me.

"Thanks for telling me," he says softly, pulling me into an embrace." I shudder against him as another wave slaps the window.

"This is how you lost them, isn't it?"

"It was a boating accident," I say. My hands are shaking, but his body is so solid against me, I'm starting to feel better being pressed up against it.

He holds me against him, not letting go.

I swallow. We shouldn't be talking about my tragic past at all. Instead, we should be talking about whether he's interested in a match with Audra and a three-way fuck with that hot bartender, but the storm raging outside right now has changed everything. My mind feels ragged.

"But it's fine," I say again, silently cursing myself for using that phrase yet again. "I mean—"

"We both know it's not really *fine*," he says softly. Then he smiles. "But I get it. That's what I say to people when they find out about my past, too. Just to change the subject for them."

He studies me for another moment, then grins. "So how about we change the subject together then? You were about to tell me more about your matchmaking before the storm interrupted us."

I watch him tentatively. He's right, I'm ready to talk about something else. He's not being insensitive; he can just read me well. "I always had a knack for it. In college, my friends were constantly pestering me to set them up," I say. "And I was pretty good at it. I thought I'd go into fashion design. But … the accident changed some things. When I finally clawed my way out of the haze after it happened, I found myself attending a few of Owen's parties. That's where I realized there were a lot of incredible, beautiful women who were struggling with dating. Especially when they were looking for something serious. That's how Match 360 started."

He nods. "Impressive. You saw a need and filled it."

"Have you ever considered being matched?" I blurt out, watching his face for the first hint of his reaction. Body language usually tells me everything I need to know, much more than words. Especially in my business.

"Who did you have in mind?" He smiles wickedly and leans forward so our faces are about six inches apart while his eyes switch from intense to playful. His hands are resting casually against my knee.

I practically bat my eyelashes at him. *Audra,* I should be saying. *My client Audra. Oh my god, what is he bringing out of me?*

"So, have you?" I ask instead.

"Depends," he answers, slightly tipping his head to one side. "Are you asking for yourself or—"

"I have a client I think you might be perfect for," I finally admit, interrupting him before he can finish. There. I've said it.

"Oh."

Shit. Unmistakable disappointment flashes across his face again just as the sky lets loose with a deafening thunderclap. Rain pelts the ship like a swarm of angry bees.

The *MaryLou* dips hard to the left and I shriek, falling against him on the bed. I quickly push myself off his body to regain my balance. Just then, I hear the door swing open behind us.

It's Owen.

20

"Cher! Are you okay?" Despite the bucking ship, Owen somehow manages to jog the length of the room and quickly pulls me into him. "I'm so sorry. The captain tried to warn me about the storm, but there were some crossed wires with the crew and I never got the message. If I'd have known, I would have gotten you off the ship before it rolled in."

"Can't we still get back to shore somehow?" I ask, horrified as the ship tips sideways to and fro.

He shakes his head. "Trying to dock right now would be too dangerous. The storm can't hurt the ship. She has the best stabilizers that money can buy to keep us upright through anything. I swear you're safe."

My mouth falls open as his words—*keep us upright*—echo through my mind. Wasn't that what they said about the Titanic?

"The coastguard says it should blow over in a few hours. I tried to tell you up on deck, but I saw you heading to your room before I could get to you." The image of him ducking under the awning with Cadence flashes through my mind. "You're safe in here," Owen repeats quickly. "You're safe."

He glances at Channing. I can tell Owen is wondering if he's just interrupted a private moment between us.

"Sorry, man. I didn't realize you would be in here," Owen says to Channing then looks back at me. "I thought I might find my girl in here having a panic attack all alone and wanted to check in on her." He turns to me. My heart beats faster. *My girl.* "I'm glad to see you're doing okay so far. It's going to be fine."

Fine never means fine.

The ship moans as it pitches to the left and we all lean hard to the right to keep from falling over. I instinctively grab onto Owen to steady myself, and he holds me tight while steadying himself against the table next to him that's fixed to the floor next to the bed. Another bolt of lightning flashes outside the wall of windows and I realize there isn't a mantra on the planet that can save me now.

Channing looks at Owen, then me, then back to Owen. I don't know what is happening behind those brooding eyes. All I know is that I wish that both men would climb under the covers with me to keep me safe and warm all night.

Channing still hasn't said a word to him since Owen arrived. It's getting a bit awkward. Owen clearly feels it too because he stands, trying to make a graceful exit. but it's impossible given how much the ship is rolling.

"Sorry to interrupt you two," Owen says, releasing his arm from my shoulders and planting his feet to stay steady. It's written all over his face that he doesn't want to leave me.

"We'll be fine," Channing finally says. "I've got her."

Owen ignores him and looks at me. "Will you be okay?"

"I'm okay," I confirm, nodding without much conviction. "Are you sure we can't get off this thing?"

"It's safer to stay here at this point," he says. "It'll all be over soon."

I swallow. I know he means it as a comfort, but it sounds ominous in my ears.

To my surprise, Owen turns suddenly back to Channing. "Will you stay with her tonight?" he asks. "If not, then I will."

They stare at each other for a moment, like two dogs ready to protect what's theirs. I don't know what's gotten into either of them. "I told Cadence I was coming over here to check on Cher, but I can let her know that I won't be coming back tonight if …" He trails off before looking back at me.

So Owen and Cadence are staying together tonight. I should have figured.

The ship pitches hard, and I'm thrown backward toward Channing. He catches me with one arm, the other holding onto the back of a leather wingback chair next to the bed that's been bolted down, swiftly steadying us both.

Still grasping onto me, Channing turns to Owen, a hint of anger laced into his voice. "I already told her that I wouldn't leave her alone tonight. Get back to Cadence. She's probably scared."

"Of course," Owen says, looking relieved. Does he hear the anger in Channing's voice? If he does, he's ignoring it. "Thanks. I'm just across the hall if you need anything."

Before he leaves, Owen leans down and takes my face in his hands—even though Channing is still holding me tight around my shoulders. "Hang in there, babe. This'll be over before you know it." Then he hurries out of my room, barely maintaining his balance.

Back to Cadence.

He's barely shut the door behind him when all the lights on the ship go dark.

21

The generator lights kicked on after a few seconds, but there's only one small spotlight hanging in the corner by my door. Which means the rest of my stateroom is still pretty dark except for the firelight trickling out of the gas fireplace on the wall opposite the bed.

A few moments ago, the captain used the backup generator to speak over the loudspeaker. He insisted we were all still safe, despite the storm raging on around us, but he demanded that everyone seek shelter in their rooms where they wouldn't fall as the ship hits pockets of waves.

With the way the ship is bucking around, Channing and I decided that the floor is the best place to wait out the storm so we aren't thrown off. At least until the *MaryLou* stops tossing us all over the sea.

He's stretched across the plush carpet on the floor beside me, the light of the fire dancing behind the glass casting a smoldering expression across his face.

Channing somehow managed to find a fifty-year-old bottle of Balvenie scotch behind the bar in my room. I'm pleasantly surprised by how much of the alcohol has stayed in my tumbler, considering how hard my hands are shaking.

"Owen sure was quick to rush in here," Channing says when we're alone and as comfortable as we can be on the makeshift bed of blankets we pulled onto the floor with us.

I take a sizable gulp of the scotch and feel the familiar warmth burn down my throat before holding the glass out to him. Our hands brush slightly when he takes it from me, and I smile in return. I could probably down the whole bottle right now and still not be able to stop my body from trembling, but at least it's starting to take the edge off.

"We've been friends for a long time," I say. My head is starting to feel fuzzy from the scotch, and the French 95 I had before that. Between that and the storm, I'm feeling reckless. Honest. Raw.

Channing takes a smaller sip from my glass as he watches me to see if I'll elaborate. I'm hoping if I push the silence long enough, he'll change the subject. I've had my fill of explaining my dynamic with Owen tonight. But he waits me out, looking at me intently with those dark eyes. I feel myself getting lost in them, pulled toward him.

Channing is for Audra, I remind myself. Not me. It's like my heart is speaking Dutch while my brain speaks German. There's no sense in what I'm doing here with him. *Get it back on track.*

"Friends?" he prods, his voice deep and scratchy after the scotch. He passes the glass back to me and I drink from the place his lips last touched while he watches. There's something so intimate about sharing a glass with someone. He poured one for us to share instead of trying to wrangle a second on the shifting floor of the yacht.

"Yep," I say simply. "He was there for me after the accident. He's the only family I have left."

He closes his eyes softly and nods like he gets it.

I move toward him so our bodies are facing each other with just a foot of space between us. "But I don't really want to talk about Owen right now," I say quietly. "Do you?"

He takes another sip from the tumbler then carefully sets it on the floor behind him, wedged into a blanket.

I'm aching for a distraction strong enough to make me forget the storm. And talking about Owen is not the kind of distraction I'm looking for.

"Do we need to talk?" he asks. His eyes burn into mine when he says it.

Electricity courses through my body, practically burning up the oxygen between us. For a moment, I can't breathe. I shouldn't do this, but I'll put my business hat back on tomorrow morning when the storm is over. Because all I can think about is how when I'm looking into his eyes, I forget for just a moment that the ship is rocking and the storm is raging.

I forget about Audra, and the promise I made to her. And most of all, I forget how I've carefully closed myself off from *this feeling* for the last decade.

Every dinner, every date, every conversation or audition I've had with men over the past ten years has been on behalf of a client. I can honestly say I've never felt this spark with any of them. I've had romantic dinners with sexy self-made million-aires and handsome world-class athletes—I've done it all—but I have never felt this burning kind of soulful energy with anyone. Not with a single one. The only person who comes close is Owen, and I refuse to let that spark ignite.

Maybe it's the storm. Or the way the dimly lit room and a shared glass of scotch between us is making me feel like I can't look away from him. Maybe it's the way he held onto me while he rushed me back to my room, or the fact that this could be my last night on earth.

Or maybe it's not really any of that at all. Maybe it's just my heart telling me it's time to open up to the possibility of feeling loved again. Maybe it's telling me to try a taste of that magical feeling I seek out for everyone else. And to finally find it for myself.

Channing brushes my hair back from my face, then takes my hands in his. If anything, his touch only makes me crave it more.

There's no mistaking it—I desperately want him for myself tonight. I want him just for me. Just for tonight. Tomorrow we can go back to playing matchmaker and matchee, but tonight I need to be just one thing: a woman clinging desperately to the man beside her.

"Channing, I—"

Before I can reply, he covers my mouth with his. His kiss is firm and soft and desperate in all the right ways. He pulls me against him, sliding me the rest of the way across the floor until there's no space left between us.

He's already hard—I can feel it through my jumpsuit. Releasing my mouth, he tilts my face back to look at me, but I'm not finished with his lips yet. I kiss him again, more urgently this time and start pulling at the button on his pants. I already know that whatever happens between us will never be enough. He starts to unzip the back of my jumpsuit, slowly at first, then faster when I don't protest.

I push him onto his back then roll on top—straddling him with my knees on the floor. For ten years, I've let the men do all the work to impress me, and now it's my turn to fuck how I want to be fucked.

I sit up taller and straighten my back so he can see me clearly. Keeping my eyes on his, I slowly pull the jumpsuit down to my navel, revealing every inch of skin beneath it. Bending at the waist while I hold myself over him, I push against his erection with my ass and lean down to kiss his mouth again. He grabs the weight of my breasts and moves his kisses down my neck, taking one hard nipple in his mouth while he pinches and rolls the nipple on the other side.

The feeling is electric as he flicks the tight coil of my nipple with his tongue, nipping expertly at it with his teeth. I groan as his erection gets even harder against me and he moans when I push back into it. He suddenly flips me underneath him, then pulls my jumpsuit down the rest of the way off my feet. He's careful not to jostle my injured foot, but it's the last thing on my mind right now.

I yank his shirt off and finally have his entire body in my line of sight. The V in his hips that I'd admired earlier on deck, leads my eyes down toward his hard shaft.

Before I can pounce on him again, Channing pushes my knees apart and dives in between, fucking me with his mouth while I fight against the screams as they mount up at the back of my throat. I can hardly hold back as I push on his hair, but I try to make this feeling, this moment last as long as I can—holding one hand over my mouth to keep myself from calling out his name. Before I can come, he hovers over top of me and rolls a condom on before plunging his shaft deep inside while kissing and biting at my neck. My entire body is so on fire. I never want him to stop.

"I want a turn on top," I breathe into his ear. And without missing a beat, he pushes his weight off me and lifts me over him so he's under me again. I ride him hard—up and down, back and forth, until Channing shudders and I shake, clenching my body desperately around him before releasing. Finally, I collapse on top of him, both of us still feverishly out of breath.

I might have just broken nearly every professional rule that I have for myself, but as the ship throws us deeper across the sea, dipping and groaning through the waves beneath us, I can't bring myself to care.

22

The storm finally seems to be backing off a little. The enormous yacht still shudders with the waves, but the worst appears to be over.

As we both come back down to earth, I feel a rush of relief.

But I don't even have time to relax before there's a knock at the door.

Channing and I look at one another from where we lay on the floor, not sure of what to do.

I grab a blanket off the floor next to us. Unsure if the door is locked, we both fumble around us for our clothes.

"Who is it now?" Channing mumbles as I pull the blanket up around my bare breasts. I have no idea who is about to enter.

"Miss Thatcher?" I hear a woman's voice shout over the wind still whipping up outside. It sounds like it might be a crew member. "Please answer if you can hear me!"

My heart races from the desperation I can hear in her voice. *This can't be good.* But the storm is getting better. What else could be happening?

"Cher? I need to come in for a minute," she calls again with more urgency.

"Yes!" I call out above the wind outside. "Please, come in!" I adjust the blanket over my chest and get to my feet, holding the wingback chair for balance. The ship is still dipping a little erratically, but it's nothing compared to the rodeo we experienced earlier.

Channing throws another blanket over the top of himself just as the door swings open.

"Miss Thatcher, you—" The crew member pauses when she sees Channing—and the plush white blanket wrapped around my naked body.

She politely looks away and starts again while bracing herself against the entry table from a sudden surge.

"I'm so sorry for the interruption." Her voice is calm and businesslike in stark contrast with the raging seas. "One of the ship's stabilizers isn't working properly. It must have been damaged by the storm. The captain is requesting everyone on deck." She chews her lip nervously before continuing.

"The deck with the lifeboats," she finishes.

23

"The lifeboats?" I hear myself ask, suddenly numb inside.

"The crew has it under control. Everything is fine," she rushes to say. "But Owen also wants you to come out there right now." She says it firmly before taking one more glance at Channing.

Everything feels like it's spiraling out of control again.

"I'm sorry," she says urgently and fear fills her eyes before she can compose herself. "There's no time to bring anything with you. Just get dressed now. Please hurry. My name is Kaylee, by the way."

"Here," Channing says, tossing me my jumpsuit from earlier. She turns her back to give us both privacy.

I get dressed in a slow-motion nightmare. The boat can't be going down. This can't be real. Channing slips his pants on as I fumble with my shoes, wincing when my hurt toe gets jostled. Within seconds, we're both decent again.

"Let's go," Channing says, pushing me toward the door.

"I brought you some flashlights," Kaylee says as she hands us heavy mag lights, then keeps one for herself. "Ready?"

I cling to Channing as we exit my room, but I can't hold back tears any longer. He's pushing me down the hallway, keeping me pressed up against him. Practically carrying me as I will my feet to obey.

We stumble our way down the dimly lit hall together with a handful of other scared-looking guests, trying to navigate the swaying ship as if we're choreographed dancers—moving and stumbling in unison—trying desperately to stay upright.

"I think I'm going to be sick," I whisper, not really caring if anyone hears me or not. Channing stops and leans next to me when I double over, cupping my face in his hands.

"Listen," he says, turning my face to his. "The storm is getting better. That's a good thing. But if those stabilizers aren't working properly, we'll be better off on deck. You won't feel as sick out there with the fresh air. And we'll also be able to—" He stops just short of finishing his thought. Before he looks away, I see something else register in his eyes. Something fearful. "It'll just be safer for us out there than in here in case we need to—"

"Almost there," Kaylee interrupts, leading the way toward the deck. Her flashlight is bouncing wildly along the hallway walls and floor as the ship continues to tip. Just before we reach deck, she pops open a compartment in the wall and pulls out life vests, handing two to Channing and a few more to the passengers around us. She straps the last vest on herself. Then she continues to lead us all toward the howling wind we can see racing past the glass window pane at the end of the hall.

"Just a precaution," she manages to say with a smile, though the smile doesn't reach her eyes. She's acting quickly and bravely, knowing we're all looking to her to lead us out, but I'm sure she's scared of what we'll find when we do reach the deck. Either Kaylee is a phenomenal liar, or she's been through enough emergency situations that she knows how to keep her calm in an unpredictable moment. Regardless, her reassurance does make me feel a little better, and I'm glad I have both her and Channing by my side.

When we get to the end of the hall, Channing stops to throw a life vest around my shoulders and snaps it across my chest like a child. I'm too scared to be embarrassed by it. Instead, I focus on following him. Not cowering back under my bed covers like every part of me is screaming to do.

When we reach the deck, I see a crowd of disheveled-looking angels and demons huddled together near the lifeboats in the wind and rain. Owen has Cadence pulled close to him while he braces himself against the rail, holding onto it with white knuckles. Next to them is Charlie Beckett, then the little devil I saw earlier who had the feather boa around her neck. She's lost her boa, and is sheltered together with her girlfriends, bracing themselves against another rail. The Victoria's Secret angels are crying, clinging to the men they came out with. All of them are missing their giant runway wings now.

When Owen spots me, he hands Cadence off to Charlie and breaks through the crowd. When he reaches me, he nearly stumbles as a rolling swell stops him in his tracks. Cadence is watching us while she clings to Charlie at the rail.

"I'm so glad to see you," he murmurs when I'm back in his arms. Owen's embrace feels so familiar, it fools my body into relaxation mode for just a moment before another rolling wave forces me to hang on to him again for balance.

"I can't do this," I say into his ear as the wind whips around us, spitting rain in every direction.

Owen pushes back strands of my hair that are flying wildly around my face, then he flashes me his bravest smile.

"I won't let anything happen to you. You know that," he says, squeezing one of my shoulders before grabbing the rail again. But the truth is, he can't control what's happening. None of us can.

"What's the plan?" Channing's voice cuts through the wind. He's still standing by my side, glaring at Owen with one hand gripping the side rail. He pulls me back from Owen, wrapping his arms around me and planting his hands firmly on the metal railing. The crowd is sheltered under an awning, but with the rain whipping from every direction, we're all soaked through and freezing.

"The crew's engineers are working on the stabilizer," he says. I clench my jaw. I had been hoping Kaylee had gotten that wrong. Owen continues. "But they're not sure how long it'll take." His voice is serious but in control. I know he's fighting to stay calm in order to keep everyone, including me, from falling apart. "We have plenty of life rafts." He stops when he looks at my face. "It probably won't come to that, but we're all staying right here just in case."

I immediately start getting tunnel vision.

Another deckhand approaches Owen from the side and says, "Sir, we need you in the control tower now. The captain requested you."

Owen turns to Channing and barks, "Don't you dare leave her side."

"Right now, sir," the deckhand yells at Owen again over the roaring wind.

He hugs me quickly one more time, kisses me on the top of my head, then pushes me back into Channing's arms. He turns to make his way toward the hallway that will lead him to the captain's control tower. Just before he hits the hall, he leans back to give me a brave smile followed by a classic Owen wink —mischievous and charming. I can't help but think he'd want that to be my final memory of him if things were to—if we were to—

I force the thought out of my mind and choke back a sob, then I bury my face into Channing's chest to block out whatever is happening around us the best I can. But before I can tune out the world around me, I spot Cadence watching me from across the deck—right where Owen left her.

If looks could kill, I'd be dead from hers already.

24

"Of all the places to have this party," Channing is muttering into the side of my head. I can barely hear him over the roar of the wind. "Why would he bring you out here, knowing what you've been through?"

"It was my idea. Owen would never—" I start to say but he interrupts me.

"He should have talked you out of it then," Channing says firmly. "He put you in the one place that he knew could destroy your sense of safety. Look at us. Look at all of us." He looks furious and wild as the wind whips around him. We're still clinging to each other near the rail while we watch helplessly as the crew preps the zodiac lifeboats.

The deck is slick with rainwater, and one guest screams as she slips. I watch in horror as she catches herself on the railing. The yacht isn't listing to the side much—not yet—but it's enough to make walking in the storm an extra challenge with each wave that slaps the side. It feels like I'm riding moguls on a ski hill. Eyeing the zodiacs, I shudder at the thought of being on a smaller boat in that water right now. I can't even think about it without wanting to throw up.

"He couldn't have known there was a storm coming," I yell back over the wind. Channing hardly knows Owen. Definitely not as well as I do. And this whole thing was my idea. "I wanted to come out here," I shout into the wind. "But—" I trail off. It's a lot to explain, and the wind is too loud.

All around us, the world's most powerful and beautiful creatures are caught in Mother Nature's fury. The storm is better than it was—but it's still one of the fiercest winds I've ever been in. Terror fills everyone's eyes each time the ship rocks with a wave. I hear a few shrieks over the sound of the water and wind churning in tandem, like a freight train bearing down on us all, made worse by the failing stabilizer. The crew handed out navy wool blankets earlier to keep guests warm on the deck, but they're all lying in heaps along the wooden slat floor, now soaking wet. Everyone is using two hands to hold onto the metal railing—or each other—like a chain link fence of human bodies sewn together across the deck.

The captain hasn't given the order yet to vacate the ship, but everyone seems to be expecting it. Cadence is holding onto Charlie Beckett, who looks like he might still be drunk from the party. Cadence's red hair is plastered all around her pale face. Even from here, I can tell she's shivering.

I force myself to look out at the water, but the view hits me like a ton of bricks and I suddenly feel disconnected from my body. Like I'm watching the scene unfold in a movie that I'm not really part of. It doesn't feel like real life. Like I'm not actually here. My grip loosens around the rail and I take a step back, fumbling to stay on my feet. Channing immediately yanks me back to him, tucking me into the space between the railing and his body again.

"Hang on to the side!" he shouts. I grip the cold steel with two hands, Channing at my back, his arms on either side of me. I study his hands near mine on the cold, hard rail. Another gust of wind sends a salty spray across my face. My knees buckle. Tunnel vision returns. Then everything disappears.

I'm on Lake Tahoe. The last rays of the sun streak across my face. Dad is at the wheel. We hurried to catch the sunset. There will be plenty of time for skiing and wakeboarding tomorrow. Mom and Ayla grin at me from the other side of the boat. Trevor puts his hand on mine. I wonder if he's forgiven me for how distracted I was on the drive here, trying to tie everything up for my senior capstone show at Fashion Week. We hit a pocket of water, and the boat pops up into the air. "Hang on," Trevor yells, grabbing onto me. He's laughing.

"Cher! Hang on to the rail!" Channing is yelling as the boat tips a little farther to the right. Somehow I've let the rail go again, and I'm clinging to Channing's body instead. He's bracing us both against the side. I manage to spin around between his outstretched arms and grab the hard metal again with both hands. I can barely open my eyes as rain slashes down all around us. Suddenly I'm back there again.

Mom scoots next to me and smooths my hair. She smiles. "Did you nail down the wedding colors?" Ayla comes to sit next to her. The boat tilts a little with the shift in weight. She's eager to hear too. I've been so busy arranging the last-minute details of my show that I haven't even finalized my wedding colors. Dad hands Trevor the wheel. He's never driven a boat. So many of my childhood memories are of Dad, smiling behind this wheel out on Lake Tahoe. I want the same for our kids. Trevor's and mine. Trevor takes the wheel from him, then turns over his shoulder. He grins back at me as he drives for a bit. He offers the wheel back to Dad and moves toward me again. The fading orange light frames his head, illuminating his golden hair. His copper sunglasses are glistening.

Just as Dad reaches for the wheel, we hit something in the water. I can't see what it is. Dad stumbles sideways, trying to keep the boat straight, but we're tipping. Trevor reaches for me. Mom grabs Ayla. Hang on, Dad shouts. The last words I'll hear him say. The boat flips hard. I'm plunged into water.

"Stay with me, Cher!" Channing is yelling behind me. "You've got this. We're almost through it." My whole body is shaking, but the ship seems to be tipping a little less. Is it my imagination? Wishful thinking? I can't tell. I can't look. I straighten my legs and shift my hands to hold the slippery metal tighter. A rogue wave, taller than the rest, surges water past the bow, forcing cold water to wash across the deck and out all of the sides again. It rushes over my feet. My mind retreats again.

I break the surface of the dark water. Tell myself to breathe. There's wreckage all around me. Breathe. *The orange flag floating.* Breathe. *A cracked ski that had been stowed on the back of the boat.* Breathe. *I scream. "Mom! Trevor!" Inhale. I dive down. Open my eyes. They burn. I reach my arms out fran-*

tically in front of me. My hands feel nothing. I see nothing. I resurface. Breathe. *Scream.* "Dad! Ayla!" *Dark, oily water slaps my face. I can't see the shore. The waves are already subsiding, the water peaceful and wrong. There should be voices, people breaking the surface. But I hear no one. I dive down again and again.*

"Cher." I hear my name.

Help me! Breathe. *They're all still under water.*

"Cher." I hear the voice again in my ear. It's Channing. He's still behind me. I crane my neck to look back at him blankly like I've just woken up from a dream. "Did you hear me?" he asks.

"What?" I feel dazed. All around us, people looking like wet rats are still holding onto the railing, but some are holding on with just one hand now. The ship is definitely rocking less than it was earlier. I'm nauseous, like I've been stuck in a hazy nightmare.

"I said I think they must have gotten something working with the stabilizer," Channing repeats. "I think we're going to be all right."

I look out at the water. It's still choppy, but almost like the plug has been pulled from the bathtub, and returning back down to normal.

The ship's PA system springs to life with a deafening shriek. The crowd startles in unison and some reach up to cover their ears. I expect to hear the captain, but it's Owen's deep voice that blasts through the speakers, cutting through the lingering gusts of wind.

"What a way to ring in a birthday, right?" His voice sounds light and airy, despite the deadly emergency we've just skirted by. I both love him and hate him for it.

A hesitant chuckle rolls through some of the guests, barely audible over the wind. I see Charlie Beckett pump his fist in the air and let out a celebratory whoop. I try blinking away my haze.

"The captain has just informed me that the crew has managed to get that stabilizer back in shape. Which is why you suddenly feel more stable on your feet." A few people let out another cheer. "We're just getting some residual waves and rain at this point, but the storm is well on its way out. So if you're feeling up to it, you're now welcome to move about the ship again as you wish." There's a slight pause. "But please stay careful."

A longer pause follows. We can hear Owen say something muffled to someone on his end. Then he comes back on to the PA. "And there will be the finest champagne flowing heavily on the dining deck, or something stronger for those of you who need it."

Charlie whoops again loudly and everyone laughs this time with more relief-filled gusto behind it. My knees go weak as I realize we're going to be okay. Channing is still bracing me up to support me.

"The power will be back on shortly, too," Owen continues.

As if on cue, the lights around us come back to life, and to more applause. A few of the guests release the railing completely and start walking off the deck toward the hallways. The ship is feeling stable again as we cut through the water. I manage to loosen my grip around Channing and the railing. A deckhand collects the life vests from everyone around us.

"Tonight was a little more exciting than we'd planned," Owen continues, sounding regretful. Then the sound of his smile streams through his voice again and I feel another rush of relief. "But we aren't going to let a little rain ruin the fun this week. Right?"

More cheers erupt from the crowd.

"Choppers won't be flying out until the morning, if you need one. But I hope you're all ready for a good time now that the storm is blowing over. I guess we have two reasons to celebrate now. See you all down on the party deck!" Another big cheer. "Signing out."

The crowd lets out a final holler, and the majority line up to hand over their life vests. I'm not ready to take mine off yet, possibly ever, but I relax my grip from around Channing and manage to take a step back from him. He glances down at me before pulling me into a tight embrace.

All I feel is relief. But before I can say anything, the captain's deeper voice comes on over the loudspeaker.

"Hi there, folks. We're heading into clearer skies and some of that immaculate Saint-Tropez sunshine for the rest of our week. Sorry about that little hiccup tonight, but I can assure you all that Mr. Hawking's vessel is secure and working perfectly again now. Your host and crew have all taken excellent care of you—"

The captain's voice is drowned out by a deafening roar from the deck as the guests begin whooping and hollering for Owen and his crew. Channing stiffens beside me.

"—rest assured you're in good hands," the captain finishes before signing off the PA system just as Cadence sidles up next to me.

"Well, holy shit," she says stiffly. She looks beautiful, even rain-soaked and shivering. "That was unreal. I need a drink." I can only nod back at her. I'm still feeling heady and dazed myself.

"Going down for a nightcap? Or calling it a night with one of the two charming men you've got hanging off you this week?" Her words lift me out of my haze and hit me like a slap across the face. She must be upset that Owen left her twice during the storm to check on me. I frown and look up at her, not sure what to say. Is that really her focus right now? After all that?

Channing gives her a quizzical look then ignores the jab, turning back toward me. "I'm calling it a night. Unless you still don't want to be alone tonight?" I search his eyes but I can't read them anymore. The desperate passion that had filled his gaze in my stateroom earlier tonight feels more like a distant memory. I haven't even processed the fact that I broke my cardinal rule with him during the storm.

"I—I think I'll head back down to my room," I stammer, feeling numb. "I'm exhausted."

Owen appears at my side. He glances between Cadence, me, and Channing.

"Want me to walk you back to your room?" Owen asks me. He must have just heard what I said. Cadence widens her eyes at me, then at Owen like she can't believe any of this. I look between all three of them and suddenly I just want to sleep.

"Why don't I walk back to my room with Channing, while you take Cadence back to hers?" I say to Owen. This conversation is suddenly a bit crowded and awkward. I'm also desperate for a hot shower and to return to my warm bed.

"My room?" Cadence scoffs. She stands in front of Owen and pulls on the front of his shirt so he's facing only her. "Your room is so much bigger though." She gives him a quick peck on the lips while I look away. "And you're not leaving my side again tonight. Cher is more than taken care of with him." She gives Channing and me a quick side glance before turning her attention back to Owen.

Owen eyes me then asks, "Are you sure, Cher?"

"Oh, for the love of God, Owen," Cadence snaps. "She's *fine*. Look at her. She's got Channing Stanbury to keep her company." Clearly the attention Owen showed me tonight hit a nerve with her. I wouldn't have pegged her for a jealous person, especially after our conversation earlier today where she seemed so at ease. But I guess I was wrong.

Music starts thumping again in the distance from the party deck. Owen must have told the crew to give the guests whatever they needed to salvage the rest of the night. I ignore Cadence's outburst and turn to Channing. "Walk me back? I think I just want to pass out now." Channing nods.

Then we turn our backs, leaving Owen and Cadence to figure out their new dynamic without an audience.

Channing keeps his arm planted firmly around me as we make our way across the deck still slick with water. I'm pretty sure I look like a wet rodent in a ruined lace jumper at this point. But I don't even care. The rest of me feels lighter and more elated than ever.

Against all odds, we survived.

25

My cell phone wakes me up early the next morning. After all the chaos of last night, I was practically asleep by the time Channing walked me back to my room. Clearly I forgot to turn on *Do Not Disturb*.

Groggily, I lift the phone to see who's calling just as Audra's name flashes across my screen.

I take a deep breath and let it out slowly before closing my eyes again and pressing the green circle.

"Morning, Audra!" I say, mustering up all the gusto I can manage.

"Cher." She already sounds testy. *Wonderful.* "Any news?"

"I made some good headway with Channing last night," I blurt into the phone. Again, it's not a total lie. I did make some serious headway with Channing last night. I just haven't exactly brought her up in conversation with him yet. But I'd rather die than mention that fact to Audra right now.

"How so?" I can tell she's distracted on her end. There's a voice talking quietly in the background and I realize she's probably still finishing her workday, given the time difference between us. She's a classic high-powered multitasker.

"Well, I think Channing's everything you're looking for," I say truthfully. I leave out the part that he's coincidentally everything *I'm* looking for, too. "His personality, looks, financial status, and his own long-term relationship goals …" I bite my lip and look up at the ceiling. I have no idea what he's looking for long-term. And he has no idea Audra exists yet. I'm teetering right on the edge of an outright lie.

"What about his ability to—" she draws out the last word instead of finishing her sentence.

"Share?" I say, picturing Channing in a three-way with Audra and another man. I chew at my lip again. "I'm still feeling that one out," I fudge. "It's a pretty unique trait you're looking for and—"

"Cher." She sighs. "I'm sorry, but you have until tonight. Then I really need to move on," she says.

I startle. "Your last text said I had until the end of the week."

"I've moved it up," she says matter-of-factly. I sit straight up in bed.

She keeps going. "My friend Brandi read a tabloid article about your work, and she's worried about me. She's been telling me to cut you off this whole time." I swallow. She's referring to Brandi Brighton, her well-known BFF and owner of a prolific gossip magazine. *Great*. Between Audra and Brandi, my failure here could become very, very public all of a sudden.

"Listen, Audra. The tabloids aren't accurate. Brandi knows that. And these things take time. We had a huge storm last night and—"

"A storm? I don't understand how a little rain could slow things down," she says impatiently.

I start talking faster. "A huge storm. It broke a stabilizer on the ship. We almost had to board the lifeboats. I was right in the middle of, um, talking to Channing when a deckhand came in and—" I take a shaky breath, feeling panicked. I don't know what else to say without sounding like I'm begging her for more time. "But the weather is back to normal today. Trust me, I'm trying my best to—" I pause and collect myself. "Listen, I'm not giving up on this. I really believe I'm making progress here."

Audra is quiet. Then, "I'm really sorry to hear that happened, but there's a reason I came to you. Your reputation, even with all the tabloid gossip, is fairly untouchable. However, this is my life, and I have to trust my gut on this. I haven't seen nearly enough—"

"You can count on me," I interrupt, hoping I sound more confident than I feel about what I'm promising. "I think I'll be able to arrange Channing's final audition—with the additional partner—tonight."

"You do?" Her voice softens just a hint.

"I do," I lie, covering my mouth and slumping back on the mattress like the words should have never escaped my lips in the first place.

"Lucky you," she practically purrs into the phone. I can tell she's at least a little intrigued by what I told her earlier. And what I'm claiming will happen tonight.

I sigh with relief knowing I have a bit more time. "Thanks for understanding, Audra—"

"Fill me in first thing tomorrow," she says curtly, then the line goes dead.

I throw the phone across my bed and pull the thick comforter up over my head.

Everything about last night still feels like a bad dream. The storm. The way things ended between Cadence and me.

The mistake I made with Channing.

And it *was* a mistake. I can see that now, in the harsh light of day, even more than I did last night. The sex was incredible, but it crossed a huge line. He still has no idea that he's my target match for Audra.

Just as bad, I'm starting to think Channing might not be the match I hoped he'd be for Audra at all. Even if I hadn't slept with him last night. Her stubborn streak mixed with what I think is jealousy between him and Owen might push him away from her desire to share. She may not be his type. But at this point, I'm desperate to salvage my contract with her. Maybe my judgment is only clouded from my feelings. From the line I crossed. And Audra isn't usually this intense. She's an incredible woman. I need to trust my instincts from before instead of letting my feelings from last night get in the way.

I'll match her with Channing if he's up for it. And if she's not happy, I'll make things right. My track record is impeccable with matchmaking successes, but everyone messes up some-times, I tell myself. Nobody is perfect.

It's still a tall order: I have no idea whether Channing will be interested in a threesome, and that's a must on Audra's list. Will he be open to sharing me or any other woman in bed? With his playboy reputation, I hope so. Aaron the Aussie bartender was certainly enthusiastic enough for all of us.

As much as I want to stay right where I am in bed for the rest of the day, I've got to get moving. As always, I start with the most basic laws of attraction. And that means making myself look absolutely irresistible, no matter how I feel inside.

26

Two hours later, my glam team has pulled together a minor miracle, stripping away any hint of stress I was hanging onto from the storm last night. Every last inch of me has been scrubbed, spray-tanned, plucked, and polished with a natural "barely there" makeup look that'll appear stunning in the natural sunlight on the deck.

Owen's stylist also hopped on a quick video call with me to pick out a shimmering gold charmeuse caftan from Marie France Van Damme that I've layered over my black Dolce and Gabbana thong bikini for a day of sunbathing out on the pool deck.

The waves are still a bit wilder than usual today, much like my hair when I woke up this morning. Owen has already ferried himself and a couple of surf buddies out to ride the bigger swells. Channing must be one of the guys who joined because I haven't heard from him yet.

As I step out into the sunlight of the deck, my head is still swimming with what happened out here last night. I'm also still trying to process everything that happened with Channing. I haven't made love to a man as just myself—not as part of an audition—since Trevor. Can I even call what Channing and I did last night *making love*? I guess that depends how he felt.

Half of me is hoping that the feelings I had for him last night were just a strange manifestation of the terror and adrenaline of the storm. I wanted so much to feel anything other than fear in that exact, awful moment. Maybe when I see him again today, I'll feel nothing for him. Maybe it was all just a stunning distraction during a time I needed it the most. If that's the case, it would definitely keep things less complicated when it comes to keeping my promises to Audra.

But … I can't stop the other half of me from feeling a little excited by the idea that my heart might be cracking open again. It felt good—so good—to have a man want me the way Channing wanted me last night. Just me. He wasn't trying to impress me just to pass an audition and be matched with one of my beautiful, successful clients. No. Everything we did, we did for ourselves. And for each other. But the thought of opening myself up to a relationship again is as scary as the idea of putting on a wetsuit and surfing the swells. I really don't know if I'm ready.

Part of me wonders if Channing knows more about my business than he lets on. Did he suspect he was being auditioned, or is he clueless to the fact that I do bedroom auditions with other men to match them with my clients?

My mind swims, and I force myself to take a deep breath. For now, I'll soak up all the sunshine and warmth while I wait for Channing to come back to the ship from the surf. I won't get any of the answers I need until then.

There's an open chaise lounge chair near the pool and I lay my thick blue-striped towel across it before stretching out. Then I slide my legs out in front of me and exhale. The hot sun baking everything around me on deck feels so grounding after last night's storm and the bone-chilling cold.

I glance out at the horizon and wait for that familiar sinking feeling to hit my gut when I take in the view. But to my surprise, it doesn't. The sight of the slow moving water feels calming—peaceful even.

But how is that possible? Especially after last night?

Then it hits me.

Of course.

Years ago, when everything was still fresh, my grief counselor had talked about exposure therapy—re-experiencing similar trauma but with a better outcome the second time around. It's supposed to push victims out of their post-traumatic cycle for a deeper recovery. When she first brought it up, I thought she was crazy. But considering the fact that I'm staring out at open water for the first time in years without any physical reaction, I'm starting to wonder if there was something to her theory.

If we survived last night, we can definitely stay afloat until the end of the week. I smile to myself. The idea of relaxing out here, being genuinely happy out on the water—it makes me feel so hopeful.

A shadow crosses my lap as Kaylee, the deckhand from last night, appears by my side. She's balancing a small tray on one hand, with a glass of lemon water for me in the other. A Tiffany-blue box wrapped with a cream ribbon sits in the middle of the tray next to a small white envelope. There's a "C" scrawled across it, making my heart skip a beat.

"It's for you," Kaylee says with a smile. Her eyes are hidden behind black aviators.

"Who is it from?" I ask, my heart beating hard. Owen? Channing? I'm not sure who would make the butterflies flutter the hardest.

She just grins and hands me the card.

As she walks away, I look at the box, then scan the deck for Owen or Channing. No luck. There's a group of surfers bobbing out in the distance on the surface of the water. Both of them must be out there somewhere.

I quickly rip open the envelope and smile when I see the familiar handwriting:

Cher,

You never fail to impress me with your strength, and last night was no exception. The sun always comes out after the rain, and I hope today feels like turning over a new leaf.

Thank you for being here, even in stormy seas.

Love,

Owen

Something stirs in my stomach while my heart swells from the words Owen wrote in his note. He has always seen me with such clear optimism, maybe more so than I've ever seen myself. Leave it to him to mark last night as an important milestone in my life. Only he would think to do that.

I reread the last line above his signature. *Love.* Smiling to myself, I place the note on the little table and lift the Tiffany box onto my lap, carefully unwrapping the ribbon before pulling off the thick blue lid.

"Oh, Owen." I grin when I see what's inside.

Nestled against the white velvet cushion is a beautiful gold leaf pendant strung on a delicate chain. He must have had this air-delivered to the ship early this morning from the nearest Tiffany store back on shore. My smile widens as I lift the necklace from the box to admire the beautiful details etched into the leaf itself.

I flip it over to see he's engraved "Your new leaf" in tiny cursive across the back.

"Do you like it?"

I jump when I hear Owen's voice so close to me. I hadn't heard him walk over, but he's standing a few feet away with his swim trunks hanging down past his navel, still dripping from the sea. The sun is bouncing off every wet muscle. "I know it's cheesy, but—"

"No, I love it," I interrupt him. My eyes are shining. "It's beautiful. And perfect. And you're right. I do feel like everything is different this morning." I study him. "How could you know that?"

A deckhand walks over to hand him a fresh towel.

"When I was up in the control tower with the captain last night, I could see you under the spotlights on deck. I could only imagine what you were going through, but you held on. You're strong as hell, Cher Thatcher." He sits at the foot of my chair and rubs the towel across his concrete abs and down his broad shoulders, each muscle rippling as he moves. I secretly wish he'd just stay wet. "How are you doing today?"

"Exhausted," I admit. "But good, too. I don't want to jinx anything, but I do feel more—" I trail off. I don't know the right word to describe how I feel about being on the water this morning. "—free." I smile to myself. "I feel almost free. Happier. Hopeful."

He stops rubbing the towel across his shoulders to grin at me. "Amazing." He pauses before adding, "Does this mean you'll join me out there for a surf?"

"Not a chance in hell," I shoot back, not missing a beat. We both laugh, fully aware I'm never going to get on a surfboard with him. No matter how good I feel this morning, sitting on a surfboard is not in my future.

"Any juicy details from last night with Channing?" He looks at me sideways, arching his eyebrows dramatically.

I nudge his shoulder but my hand just slides off his slick skin. He laughs again and pats the towel down each arm, easily passing for a model posed on the helm of a yacht without even trying.

"I'm still trying to figure that out. We—" I pause, hesitant to say it out loud. But I tell Owen everything. "—we made love last night during the storm."

Owen pauses the towel midway down one arm and looks at me hard.

"Before we were all called out on the deck. Right before the stabilizer went out," I say.

"He already got to the final audition?" He's leaning toward me now on the chair, and his focused reaction is making me squirm. I've never used the term "made love" to describe my auditions with potential matches. Ever. And of course he's picked up on that.

"No," I say slowly. "*I* slept with him. *Me.* Not as a matchmaker. Not as part of an audition. He still doesn't even know that Audra exists. He has no idea that I'm trying to match him with a client."

He tosses his towel to the side, studying my face like he doesn't know what to say. There's something about Channing that seems to have gotten under Owen's skin. And vice versa.

I don't know what to say either, so I start fumbling with the gold necklace, trying to clasp the hook behind my neck.

He suddenly looks thoughtful. "Well, I guess that new leaf has two meanings now, doesn't it?" He's staring at me like he can't believe it. "I've been waiting a long time to see you ready to open your heart up again, but I never saw it coming with someone like Channing." His brows knit together.

Owen rises to stand behind me. He sweeps my hair off my shoulders, letting his hands brush my collarbone as he takes the clasp from between my fingers.

Owen has fastened necklaces for me a hundred times before. It should take a few seconds at most, but this time he lingers, still holding the necklace, standing out of my sightline. Then, ever so slowly, he trails his hands along the tender spot beneath my ears, and finally clasps the tiny chain. Then he gently sweeps my long hair down behind my shoulders, letting it cascade across my back again. The whole thing sends a sequence of shivers down my spine.

I absentmindedly touch the leaf pendant hanging just below my throat. Owen steps around me and sits at the foot of my chaise lounge. I physically ache for him to touch me again, even if it doesn't mean anything more than what he's just done. I want it so badly it hurts.

I stare at his hands, unable to meet his eyes. He's leaning in, bent at the waist, and I can feel him beckoning me to look up at his eyes. When I finally raise my eyes to meet his, he breaks into a soft smile.

"The new leaf looks good on you," he says, and I feel myself flush. Then his eyes narrow again before he asks, "What was it about Channing last night that … you know, changed things for you?"

The question hangs thick in the air between us, his turquoise eyes boring into mine so intently, I don't notice someone else approaching us.

"I can't put my finger on it," I say truthfully. "I'm not even sure I—"

"Cher." Someone interrupts me before I can figure out how to explain to Owen.

I look up to see Channing casting a shadow over us both.

27

"Hey, man!" Owen says heartily, breaking the heavy silence. He stands and slaps Channing across the shoulder with a welcoming smile. I'm left admiring his ability to break the ice between them yet again. Owen can exude enough warmth to melt a glacier when he wants to. We're both good at playing the part we need to play, I think, remembering back to my conversation with Cadence yesterday over breakfast.

"Hey," Channing says with a tight smile.

If Owen notices Channing's curtness last night and this morning, he doesn't show it. "I was just taking off to get myself put back together after that gnarly surf session this morning. That storm really brought in some good waves," he says casually, then grabs the towel lying on the deck and hangs it loosely around his shoulders. "Planning on joining us out there again tomorrow morning for another surf sesh before you take off?" He looks expectantly at Channing.

"I'm not sure yet," Channing says, first looking at Owen and then at me. "If it's a late night, I might pass."

I see a hint of a smile on his face and can't help mirroring it.

"Gotcha. I'm going to go shower off." Owen smiles a knowing smile at both of us, and I curse him for being so awkward right now. *Just be cool, Owen.* "Enjoy this incredible sun today. Hope it makes up for last night. I'll catch you both later for dinner then, yeah?"

"Yeah, sure," Channing replies, less ice to his voice this time.

Before he disappears into the hallway tunnel, he turns to Cadence who's just made her entrance onto the pool deck. She looks stunning once again in a creamy crocheted sundress over a neon blue string bikini. She smiles at Owen and waves, then stops when she sees me. No doubt wondering if I'm the one he's walking away from.

I sigh and wave at her halfheartedly. I seem to be adding a lot of drama to Owen's love life right now, and him to mine. Channing and I aren't even in a relationship, but it's hard to miss the fire in his eyes whenever Owen is around. Which means he's probably not into sharing at all.

Ugh.

Channing smiles and sits on the lounge next to me before kissing me on the cheek. "Were you able to sleep last night after—" He stops when he sees the empty Tiffany box on the table next to me. Then his eyes land on the only piece of jewelry on my body—the new necklace glistening around my neck.

"From Owen?" He gestures at the necklace.

"Yes," I say, "but it's not what it looks like." *Why did I feel the need to say that?*

"Tiffany's, huh?" He raises his eyebrows at me before staring out at the horizon of waves like he's accepting defeat. He hasn't even heard me out yet. This whole jealousy thing isn't going to work for me. Or for Audra's sole 360 request.

"It's … for what happened last night." I shrug. "I made it through the storm. Everything feels different today. I've turned over a new leaf." I make air quotes around "new leaf" as I watch his jaw start to soften.

He turns to me with his eyes suddenly full of curiosity. "You faced your fears. Exposure therapy," he says.

I stare back at him, surprised that I don't have to explain.

He takes my hand, but he must notice the look on my face because he adds, "Don't forget, I have a past too." The space around his eyes crinkles up when he smiles.

I nod. Channing knows what I've been through. I squeeze his hand and smile back at him, then look down at the leaf necklace. "It has a double meaning to me though," I say, treading carefully.

"And what's that?" he asks, reaching out to touch the necklace gently. The heat of his hand next to my collarbone reminds me of last night, giving me courage to say what I want to say to him.

"Opening up. To you," I say slowly. "I haven't done that in a long time."

His dark eyes settle heavily into mine. "So Owen gave you that necklace to commemorate us—" He pauses, finishing his own question by raising his eyebrows slightly.

I laugh. "No. He's just saying he's proud of me."

"Huh," Channing says, squinting his eyes. "Well … that's nice of him. I know you said he's like a brother … but I've never heard of a brother like that." There's a smile breaking through his sarcasm.

I roll my eyes. "Owen is Owen. He will always be Owen. But I want to talk about us," I interrupt him.

Smiling, he leans in to kiss me.

As his lips meet mine, I remember my phone call with Audra this morning and slowly pull back. I might have turned over a new leaf last night by opening up my heart, but I also crossed a line. My biggest line. I'm committed to auditioning him for Audra and giving their relationship a real chance. Last night felt so real, so important. But I tell myself it's not because Channing is *the one*. It's because I finally realized that I'm not broken after all. Not when it comes to my heart, not when it comes to anything.

"I need you to know that I've never actually done this before," I finally blurt out. "I've never slept with someone I'm trying to set up with a client."

He sits up straighter, looking confused. And rightfully so. *Oh, god. I've already messed this up.*

"No, that's not true. Let me rephrase that. I actually sleep with most of the men I'm setting up with a client." *Oh my god, that came out totally wrong.*

He looks even more confused. Horrified, really.

"Okay, wait, let me start that over."

"Hold on. You're trying to set me up with a *client*?" he asks. His confusion is quickly turning into disappointment—edging on anger.

"I thought maybe you knew more about my business than you were letting on …" I say weakly.

"Are you serious? And are you saying that all of this was just a ruse to get closer to me so you could just set me up?"

"No! Well, at first, yes, but just hear me out," I plead, putting both hands up, trying to stop his thoughts from snowballing. "I do have a client that I'm trying to set you up with."

His face instantly hardens, tension screaming into his jawline and eyes. I start talking faster. "Her name is Audra. She's incredible. Beautiful. Smart. Successful. Knows exactly what she wants. Anyone would be lucky to be with her—that's the only kind of client I take on," I ramble. "At first, I was just trying to get your attention to try and—"

He interrupts me again. "So you want to pass me off to someone I don't even know, someone I don't even care for, just because she's 'smart and beautiful'? You were just pretending to be interested in me last night to match me with another woman as part of some business scheme?"

"No!" I answer. "And it's not a scheme. Last night was real. That's what I'm trying to tell you. That was about me. Not Audra. It was a mistake—"

"A mistake?" A flicker of hurt crosses his features.

"Not like that," I rush to say. "Just listen, I know this is a lot—"

"Are you still trying to match me with her?" he asks abruptly. "With this Audra woman?"

"Yes, but please just listen."

He finally falls silent, turned sideways on the chair, facing the pool now instead of me. I don't know how to explain this, so I just come out with the full truth.

"I broke my cardinal rule by being with you last night. And I don't take that lightly." I'm frustrated with myself for explaining this so poorly, but he's hardly let me get a full sentence out. I exhale slowly, trying to collect my thoughts before continuing.

"Last night, the storm stirred a lot of things up for me," I begin again.

"You can't blame how we felt about each other last night on the storm," he says. His gaze darts down to my necklace and I realize I'm fingering the chain again without meaning to. I quickly put my hands back down in my lap. I wish I could start this whole conversation over.

"Audra would be perfect for you," I say too loud, dumping the words into the air between us then holding my breath— waiting for the aftermath to crash in. It's true. She would be. My initial gut reaction was right. And she would absolutely love this man in front of me. More than I ever could.

I wait for Channing to react, positive that I've ruined everything.

Instead of blowing up at me, he turns away and rests his elbows on his knees, head bent toward the deck like he's studying something in the wooden slats. I almost wish he had fired something back at me instead of simply looking down or defeated—letting the silence hang between us.

"So last night *wasn't* an audition for your client—but you still want to hand me off to your client?" He squints up at me, like he's staring into the sun.

"I—I do like you, Channing, but I think you should give Audra a chance. Last night was incredible, but that's all I have to give you right now."

I take a deep breath to collect myself again, looking away from him and pushing away any memory of last night. I take another deep breath and rein in my years of experience matching the most elite, the most finicky, the most particular people in the world. Then I exhale slowly and look at him. Before my resolve wavers again, I continue.

"She's incredible, Channing. Besides being absolutely stunning, she is successful and—and strong," It's all tumbling from my mouth like an awkward sales pitch. I match elite clients with knife-like precision, but I suddenly feel like I've morphed into a clumsy newbie grasping at sales leads. A solid reason to never allow myself to cross this line with a potential match again.

"Give Audra a chance," I whisper.

His eyes search mine again, as if he's trying to understand my plea.

I focus hard not to give anything away through my eyes.

"She's better for you than I am," I say, almost convincing myself with the conviction I hear in my voice. *Almost.* "This is my job, remember? I have a sixth sense for these things."

There's a long pause as the ship rocks us gently back and forth. A few more guests are gathering on the deck. Our moment out here alone together is wearing thin. Cadence and another model are pulling their sundresses up over their heads to lather each other up with sunscreen as they get ready to take a dip in the pool.

"That's really how you feel?" Channing finally breaks the silence.

I nod.

He shakes his head like he's fighting against himself. Nearly smiling, but not quite. He's coming around to the idea, which makes my stomach sink and soar at the same time. What we shared together last night must not be that difficult for him to push aside in the name of finding a real match with Audra.

He sighs. "I can't believe I'm asking this, but what would this official match look like? Do I just go out with her when we get back?"

Here we go. I switch on my most professional voice and explain the process just as I've explained it dozens of times before.

"I'm satisfied with my analysis on your personalities and the other factors at play. I think you and Audra would complement each other well. To complete the match, I'll need to find out how you two would match sexually." I watch every twitch of his face to see how close we are to closing this deal. He shifts on the chair we're sharing, his cheeks flushing ever so slightly.

He breaks into nervous laughter. "Oh my god, this is too much." I wait for the inevitable to click in his mind, with what I blurted out earlier. "Wait, do you do this with every potential match?"

I raise my eyebrows at him.

My silent answer.

"You really sleep with every guy you set your clients up with?"

"Not every guy. Just the ones I'm confident will make a good match. And only if I've been asked to do a Full 360 Audition. Which, to be honest, is kind of what's made me famously unique. And wildly successful."

He studies my face, looking for the pending joke. When he accepts that there isn't one coming, I explain the full process to him. I don't hold anything back anymore. I won't mislead him again. To his credit, he doesn't look completely horrified when I'm finished. Just a little shell-shocked.

"But Audra's preferences are … not completely *typical*," I say, pushing ahead. He shifts in his seat again. "And last night won't really do her contract justice."

"What do you mean by 'not completely typical'?" Hunger and desire fill his eyes. "If last night wasn't enough then—"

I take a deep breath.

"She wants her partner to be open to a *ménage à trois*," I say quietly. Thankfully, the other guests across the deck are so wrapped up in their own conversations that no one seems to be listening to us.

I look back at Channing and lower my voice again before continuing. "Her match has to be open to another man being in the bedroom. Not for *you* to touch or kiss, per se. But you would have to be okay with another man having sex with me during the audition, while you participate. The same would be true for any future sex you might have with Audra as well."

Channing swallows hard and studies me.

"She's looking for someone who's confident enough in the bedroom that they're willing to share," I finish.

There.

I've said it.

My heart is beating out of my chest as I watch my proposal sink in.

28

"So, it would be you and I sharing a bed again—but with another man?" he asks slowly.

"That's right," I confirm, fighting to keep my focus.

I watch him, praying he'll accept. "Then giving a relationship with Audra a real chance when it's over. Without me involved."

I chew my lip as we look into each other's eyes. I'm sure I'm mirroring the internal struggle he's working through in my own expression, too.

"Is this really what you want?" he asks quietly.

I nod firmly. Maybe I'm ready to open my heart up again, maybe I'm not. But whatever happened between us last night is in the past. Right now, I need to focus on Audra and their potential relationship. I now have a clear picture of why I never let myself get romantically wrapped up in a potential match. It threatens everything.

"Tonight," I say. "And I already have someone in mind for the third person, if you'll just say yes."

"Owen?" he asks as his eyes narrow darkly.

I can't help it. I burst out laughing. "I told you. That's not how things are between us."

"You haven't even been *his* matchmaker?" he asks.

"Never," I confirm. But the thought of those two men locked on either side of me is like a dream come true. My body starts pulsing just thinking of it.

"Is it Coz?" he asks.

"No." I laugh again, remembering our first time meeting in the hallway with Coz the other night. "He's been moved on to his official match with Zara Cordon."

He looks like his head is spinning. "Okay then … who do you have in mind?" He finally gives me a tentative smile.

I grin at him. We're almost there.

"The Aussie behind the bar."

Channing lets out a hearty, unexpected laugh, breaking up the mounting tension between us.

"The *bartender*?"

"He's the one." My smile widens. "No strings attached is the best way to do this. He was completely onboard when I floated the idea of a threesome by him the other night."

A flash of surprise crosses his expression again, but it's gone so fast I think maybe I imagined it.

"Does Aaron know that I'm the potential third wheel?" Channing asks, looking surprised that I've been planning this as long as I have. I can't tell if he is flattered or hurt that this whole charade has been mounting—without his knowledge—the entire time we've been aboard the *MaryLou.*

"I pointed you out to him at the Fallen Angels party last night before the storm picked up."

"Jesus Christ," he mutters under his breath. "I had no idea you were this kind of mastermind."

I smile at him while he starts rubbing his jaw. "Ta-da?" I say with a grin.

He sighs. "I don't know whether to be flattered or pissed."

"Be flattered," I say. "Just be flattered and enjoy the ride." I smile at him suggestively. Then, in order to seal the deal, I add, "So can I count on you for tonight?"

When our eyes meet, it's all there: confusion, excitement, and above all else, an intense desire. He swings one leg over the other side of the chaise so he's straddling the chair, finally facing me just inches away.

He plants both hands on my knees and caresses my bare skin, studying my face as he does. Then he runs one hand slowly down to my foot, raising up the toe I injured last night. "You're healing nicely," he says, like a doctor examining a patient.

"I had someone taking good care of me." I smile at him. We've come a long way since the accident on the dance floor. I know he's buying time, avoiding the question at hand, but I'm enjoying the feeling of his touch anyway. If he needs a minute to consider what I've offered, that's fine. I'm just grateful he hasn't run the other way yet.

He cups my foot in his palm and plants a kiss on the top of my toe ever so gently, conjuring up the intimacy we shared last night when neither of us were sure whether or not we'd see the morning.

He takes a deep breath. "Tonight then." He raises his eyebrows at me, confirming what I thought might be impossible. My stomach hits the deck, but somehow I play it cool.

"Tonight," I confirm, raising my eyebrows back at him. "Come to my room at ten p.m. I'll let Aaron know the plan. And I'll also let Audra know you're moving on to the final step in the audition."

He looks uncertain when he hears her name, but quickly masks it with a nod.

I pull my foot back from his hands and brush his cheek with my palm so he'll look up at me.

"See you tonight," I whisper, then I lean in and gently kiss him on the cheek, just at the edge of his lips.

Then I pull away and briskly walk across the deck without turning around.

29

It's the final night aboard the *MaryLou*, and Owen has spared no expense in transforming the mega-yacht for the biggest night of the week, maybe the year. Helicopters have been steadily ferrying new, powerful guests aboard the ship all day for this last bash, since many of Owen's friends could only spare one night from their busy lives and chose to join the grand finale of the week.

There's a long lineup of Grammy-winning artists ready to serenade the crowd all night long and every deckhand aboard the ship is running at full speed to keep even the most high-maintenance guests happy throughout the day leading up to the big night.

Charlie has been floating on a huge, overinflated pink flamingo in the infinity pool all day being handed one umbrella drink after another. And I'm pretty sure I saw four of the runway models from last night jumping naked off the side of the ship when a skinny dipping party broke out. Even the generally serious talk show host billionaire, Hazel Riverton, looked a little tipsy talking to her tiny dog on deck after lunch was over.

Given the growing crowd, it's not hard for me to avoid Channing for the rest of the day. I'm sure that any minute he's about to appear over my shoulder to tell me that he's gotten cold feet. That tonight is off.

Surprisingly, I have never been asked to complete a ménage à trois as part of a Full 360 Audition before, so this will be my very first time. I've never been this nervous, and it doesn't help at all that one of the men is Channing. But I keep reminding myself that I'm not there to impress anyone. The opposite, actually. I'm still pinching myself that I've managed to pull this off.

I asked a crew member to deliver a sealed note to Aaron the bartender, telling him to meet me in my room at ten p.m. for the rendezvous we'd discussed the other night. I had her put a spare key to my room in the envelope as well so we can forego that particular awkwardness.

All that's left to do now is get through the afternoon without any more hiccups.

Two hours earlier, I asked Owen's stylist to help me plan my look for tonight. We chose a gorgeous Coco de Mer red thong teddy set to wear under my curve-hugging scarlet-red vintage Chanel dress for the evening.

"My god, Cher, you're going to make me rethink liking women," his stylist had crooned into the speaker when I'd held it up to my screen. By the time our call ended, my stomach felt like it was housing an army of butterflies. I can't stop imagining Channing and Aaron watching me take everything off later at the exact same moment.

Now I'm standing in my dressing room adding the final touches to my look before heading out to the party. I've already strapped myself into the delicate red teddy, so all I have left to do is slip on my dress and shoes. Just as I'm sliding on the pair of nude Manolo Blahnik sandals, I hear the door to my room open. I must have forgotten to lock it again.

"Just a minute!" I call out from the dressing room. I'm guessing it's Owen. I haven't put the Chanel dress on over the lingerie yet, and this tiny, sheer teddy shows all the parts of me that Owen has yet to see. I pause for a fraction of a second, imagining what he might do if I simply walked out of the dressing room in this see-through bodysuit instead of throwing on my dress like I normally would. I stand in front of the mirror in my closet for one brazen moment, seriously considering it. Then my logic surfaces and I decide against it.

Someone speaks behind me just as I'm reaching for my dress.

"Hello there, darlin.'"

I spin around at the sound of Coz's deep Southern accent and quickly grab my dress from the hanger to hold it up tightly against my body. There's barely enough fabric to cover the thin drape of material between him and my body.

"Coz, what the hell are you doing in here?" I hiss, my voice searing the air. Coz toed the line earlier this week, but coming into my dressing room without an invitation is the last straw. I'm completely vulnerable in here.

"Apparently I'm comin' in at just the right moment." He's slurring his words, and his eyes are scanning my body, taking in every inch of my exposed skin. I struggle to stretch the red dress across both my crotch and my breasts, barely covered by the red negligee underneath. He's drunk. I can smell alcohol on his breath. So strong it's likely oozing out of his pores, too. "Get out," I say firmly. Standing a bit straighter, I shove him hard toward the door, holding the dress up with my other hand, but he doesn't budge.

There's no way I can match him with Zara after this.

"Whoa, whoa." He puts his hands up like I have a gun drawn on him, and I wish I did. "No need for embarrassment, honey. Are you forgetting how familiar I already am with—with this?" He trails off as his eyes drip down my body again with a low whistle. "But this little red thing you have on tonight is really something special. Why weren't you wearing something like that for me the other night?" He staggers backward, but regains his footing before taking another step toward me.

Before I can react, he reaches out and fingers the top of the teddy near my breasts.

I smack his hand away, taking a step back. The dressing room suddenly feels too small with him taking up this much space between me and the door.

"You need to leave," I repeat firmly. There's no way I can set him up with Zara—but maybe I can use that reminder to get him out of here. "You're already promised to Zara, remember? Get out before you do something stupid. *Now.*" I shove him again, but he responds by moving toward me instead of the door.

"Zara won't mind. She didn't care if you slept with me once. She won't mind another rodeo." He pretends to pout and my gut recoils. "I promised I'd be a good boy *after* I'm with her. But until then …"

He reaches for me again to pull at the edge of the dress I'm holding up across my body, but I jerk away from him.

"Go," I say louder and shove him again. He smiles like he's amused that I can't move him on my own. He stands like a rock, and it's clear I can't budge him myself.

"I know you enjoyed yourself the other night." He reaches out to touch me again on the neck. "Your whole body told me so. We're going to do that again, honey."

I smack his hand away as my entire body goes cold. I'm doing everything I can to look fierce against him, but my legs tremble as he moves in closer.

"That's right, honey," he says, eyeing my lower half. "Shake for me again." How did I misread him this badly? I've never seen Coz this drunk before. What a huge shift in his character.

I glance between him and the door. There's a red emergency button on the other side of that wall. It's part of the keypad, but I'd never make it. He'll swipe me up with one enormous paw if I try to sprint around him right now.

"Go!" I say even louder, nearly shouting. The sound of my own shaking voice sends goosebumps down my legs. "Get out of here!"

Suddenly he lunges at me, grabbing at my shoulders like he's going to try to kiss me, then clumsily pushes himself against me so my back is against the wall. I move my face away from his and start screaming at him, clawing his chest.

"Get off me!" I fight him with all of my strength but it's no use. He's too big.

Click.

I hear the door open.

Half a second later, Owen appears at the doorway. His face is red with anger when he sees Coz braced up against me.

I feel dizzy with relief.

Owen grabs one of my heels off the rack. He reels back and whacks it across the back of Coz's head. The heel flies off from the force, and Coz spins around looking stunned long enough for Owen to knee him in the gut, then hit him across the face.

Horrified, I watch Coz nearly trip over another shoe as he lunges at Owen. No way I can stop him myself. I race to the keypad on the other side of the door and slam the red panic button, then rush to the dressing room just in time to see Coz slam Owen into the wall.

I scream again, but Owen pushes off the wall and rams into Coz, making him stumble toward the wall.

Within seconds, a team of security rush in, and together they all manage to wrestle Coz to the ground.

3 0

Coz protests, still slurring his words as the security team leads him out the door. "We were just having a little fun, gentlemen. She'll tell you that herself, right, Cher?" His words make me sick.

They'll be back to take my statement once they have him secured in another area of the ship.

Owen keeps his arm protectively around me while they lead Coz away.

I consciously force my breath—and heart rate—to slow to a normal pace. I'm still holding my dress up against my body like a shield, just like I'd done when Coz first arrived.

Owen removes his ripped suit jacket and brings it gently around my shoulders. Then he pulls me into a hug. I'm still only wearing the teddy underneath the jacket now draped around my shoulders, but I don't care what I'm wearing—or not wearing. I just want to feel the security and familiarity of his arms, so I lean into him, hugging his waist.

His heart pounds against my chest. Under different cir-cumstances, this type of scantily clad embrace might have been a dream come true for me. But right now, his presence is grounding me again after what's just happened—better than anything else I could ask for.

After a minute, he loosens his embrace around my waist, but I take it as a cue to tighten mine. I'm not ready to let go of him yet. He feels me wrap my arms harder around him, and he slowly does the same. I take another shaky breath with my head against his chest and close my eyes. If only we could stay like this forever.

"Hey," he says, resting his cheek against my head. He's still breathing heavily from the fight. He rubs my back up and down while I let my body melt into his. "Are you okay?" He pulls my shoulders back just enough that he can look into my eyes without exposing the rest of my body. There's still venom in his eyes, as he fights to regain control, and he pulls me back into him. "I'm going to fucking kill that guy."

"I didn't know he was coming here," I stutter. "It's—it's my fault. I must have left the door unlocked. You were right about that. It's my fault. And—"

"Nothing about that was your fault," he says firmly. He sits me down on the edge of my bed and pulls his suit jacket more tightly across my shoulders. Then he finds my robe on the back of a nearby chair and holds it out to me. I don't move to take it.

"Do you want to put this on before the security team gets back?" I nod at him without making eye contact, but I don't move to take the robe from his hands. He sets it on my lap.

Owen moves in front of me, where I sit on the edge of the bed. He gently takes hold of the suit jacket resting across my shoulders and starts to pull it down.

He keeps his eyes glued on mine, then slips the suit jacket the rest of the way off my shoulders. He's so close, I can feel his warmth against my skin. Then he gently slides the robe's sleeve over my wrist, up my arm and onto my bare shoulder.

He pauses, never letting his eyes move from mine while I sit practically naked in front of him. Despite what's just happened, I feel completely safe in this moment.

Our eyes stay on one another, and for one agonizing moment, I think he might kiss me. But he pushes his forehead against mine instead. So close, I can almost taste his mouth as our breath mingles into the tiny slice of air between us.

His lips part and I close my eyes.

He leans in closer.

My heart thuds harder.

Then his lips brush mine, ever so slightly. So gently I barely feel them. But neither of us move to close the gap between us.

I feel him smile against my lips as they graze mine one more time, light as the tip of a feather. I'm so hungry for him, I nearly pull him into me.

Just as I'm about to grab him to close the space between us, he speaks.

"If this is too much after what just happened—" He pauses. I don't move, and neither does he.

"It's not," I whisper back, my eyes still closed. Our lips brush again, and I silently wonder if he can hear my heart thumping out of my chest. But the moment feels like it's slipping away when he pushes back from me slightly. I bite my lip and hold my breath.

But, just like that, my heart cracks open as he briefly pulls away.

He shakes his head. "I'm sorry. The crew is on their way to get a police statement from you. I don't know what I was thinking—"

"Owen, don't—" I start to say, but now that he's farther away in front of me, I can see he's starting to fume again as he thinks about what just happened.

"When I walked in and saw Coz on you—" His voice catches and he stops to pull away from me entirely. He's not even trying to mask his anger, and I can tell he's going to make sure Coz's life is hell until he can get him off the ship.

"Will you tell me what happened?" he asks, turning around to face me.

"It's fine," I say briskly. There's that word again. *Fine*. It's not fine, but it's over, and I don't want to think about it anymore. I'd rather get back to whatever was just happening between Owen and me. "I misjudged Coz. But I'm okay."

Owen gives me an incredulous look. "It's fine? If I hadn't come in when I did ..."

"But you *did* come in when you did. Nothing too awful happened." I don't know why I feel the need to downplay it, but the whole thing feels humiliating. I'll give my statement to security so they can deal with him, then I want to leave it all behind me.

"He could have really hurt you."

"I'll tell security what happened. They'll deal with it," I say firmly, then pivot. "Are you okay? Did you get hurt?"

He ignores my attempt at changing the focus back to him. His eyes soften. "I'm okay. And you don't have to talk about it. What I'm trying to say is … when I think about you getting hurt, it tears me up. You mean too much to me, Cher. I've always thought we might …"

But he won't finish the sentence.

"Always thought we might what? Owen?" Suddenly I'm furious. "Spit it out. What was that a second ago?"

He stares at me. He opens his mouth, then closes it again, clenching his jaw. I'm so mad I could scream.

"We've been friends for well over *ten years*. Ten years that you could have tried to do something like that. And you wait until this exact moment—to what? To confuse the hell out of me?"

His jaw flexes as he tries to form a response.

"Why Channing?" he asks, his voice deep and serious. "What is it about him that makes you feel like you could open your heart up to him? After all this time? Why him?"

"I don't know!" I respond truthfully, exasperated. "Why do you care?" I'm giving him an opening right now. To say whatever it is that he was trying to say a moment ago, before pulling away from me.

"I've always cared." His eyes are shooting out a lifetime of emotions at me. "More than you know. But Channing walks in this week and suddenly the walls come down? Why?"

He's asking me to bare my heart. Is that what he wants to hear? Does he feel the same way I do? I still don't know. But I can't forget the last time I misread his signals—and I won't make that mistake again.

"I'm still trying to match Channing with Audra tonight." I force the words out, angrily.

"You're finishing his audition tonight?" he asks in disbelief. "But what about—"

"It's better for everyone," I say curtly. I've never felt so angry with him.

Just then, the security team comes in. They look between Owen and me, and I'm sure they can sense the tension that's just filled the room.

The head of security clears his throat.

"What's the status?" Owen asks, forcing the pained look to drain from his face.

"Coz is on his way back to shore for booking, pending your statements."

We both breathe out a sigh of relief.

"We just have a few questions for you, and then we'll let you get back to your evening," the officer says, looking at me.

"Good," I say firmly. "Because I have work to do."

31

Owen leaves as soon as we give our statements to the head of security.

I think he half-expected me to fly home early—instead of finishing my audition with Channing tonight. I didn't press to finish our conversation. I need to get through tonight before I can even think about diving headlong down that rabbit hole.

But I can't help wondering. Does he actually have feelings for me? Have I gotten it wrong all this time? Is this because of what happened with Channing last night? What kind of timing is that?

I push the questions away. I'm actually looking forward to my night ahead with Channing and Aaron. If anything is going to help me forget the roller coaster of the last couple hours, it's going to be a night sandwiched between those two.

* * *

Over an hour later, once I finish giving my statement to security and my glam team has me fixed back up, I'm ready to try this again. It's the final night on the *MaryLou,* and I'm going to own this ship.

I pull Owen's stylist up on a video chat to have him pick out a new outfit for the night: a shimmering gold Oscar de la Renta cocktail dress over a delicate ivory Kiki de Montparnasse bodysuit underneath. The old outfit felt cursed for more than just my run in with Coz. I'll never be able to wear it again without remembering the look Owen gave me right before his lips touched mine—once, twice, three times.

Back on deck, a slick-looking vocalist serenades the crowd as a slight breeze sweeps past the sun setting over the water. The golden rays of the sunset are shimmering off the waves.

I run my fingers over the necklace Owen gave me this morning. This trip has turned over a new leaf for me in so many ways. I'm not broken. I'm not doomed to keep my heart locked up tight. No matter what happens tonight, I'll be forever grateful to Channing for making me feel capable of that again.

While I gaze out at the railing, Owen comes to stand next to me. He looks down at me with a smile, and I smile slowly back up at him.

God, we're complicated. But even if we have one of the most complex friendships on the planet, I'm still happy to be here with him. He links his arm in mine and we both lean into each other. I put my head on his shoulder as we stare out at the sunset together over the water.

"I like how that new leaf looks on you," he says to me without glancing over. He smiles again, but still doesn't meet my eyes. The golden sunbeams sinking into the horizon are lighting up his face, making his eyes look almost translucent against the sunlight. "I'm sorry about earlier," he says. I squeeze his arm and admire his familiar profile. The wind lightly tosses his hair as his skin radiates the sun's last warmth of the day.

"I'm not," I say quietly.

He squeezes me back, looking over at me with a smile. I exhale and close my eyes, letting the wind sweep across my face as I breathe in the sultry sea air. There's nowhere else I'd rather be.

"Hey, you two," Cadence says, suddenly behind us.

I pop my head up and loosen my grip on Owen's arm.

"Hey, Cadence," we say in unison, then look at each other with a faint smile. *Jinx.*

"Hardly an inch between you two anytime I see you!" she says, missing the mark with her sarcasm so it comes out a little bitter. Insecure.

Cadence looks stunning in a shimmering white mini-dress that shows off her impossibly long legs and Saint-Tropez glow. She is every inch a supermodel, with a certain curve to her face that you can't quite put your finger on, making it hard to look away from her.

Owen would be lucky to have her.

He slowly unhooks his arm from mine and gives Cadence a peck on the cheek. She glances in my direction triumphantly before leaning into him.

"You look beautiful tonight," he says to her.

"Same to you, birthday boy," she purrs as she stares into his eyes, then kisses him squarely on the lips.

I look away and quietly excuse myself, ignoring the tiny dagger in my chest. Nothing has really changed between Owen and me, even though the moment we just shared in my room makes me question everything. *You're auditioning Channing with Aaron tonight,* I remind myself. *Focus on that.*

I spot Aaron behind the nearest bar. He's tossing around a metal cocktail shaker with a huge smile plastered across his face. He points to himself then erupts in laughter along with another guest. He is absolutely delicious to watch. *This is going to be fun,* I remind myself, picturing him and Channing curled around me later on.

I leave Cadence and Owen to watch the rest of the sunset alone together. Aaron sees me watching him and gives me a quick wave. I can already tell from the look on his face that he's still absolutely on for tonight.

"Hey, there," I say, sidling up to his countertop. "Fancy seeing you here."

"Hello there, gorgeous," he says in that rugged Outback accent. I've never slept with an Australian before, but I hear they can be pretty bold—which is exactly what we're going to need to get through a night like this. I'm looking forward to the distraction.

"We've got a date later tonight," I say back with a wink. "Still up for a little get-together?"

"Are you kidding me?" He laughs, twisting a bottle open with a snap of his wrist. The muscles ripple down his arm as he passes the bottle to the guy next to me. A shot of electricity goes through me at the thought of him kissing me later on with Channing in the room. "I'm thrilled you asked me to join."

I blush slightly as he asks if I'd like anything to drink.

"A French 95, please," I say. "The last one you made me was amazing."

"No Coors Light? Okay, Miss Class," he says with a smirk. Then he presses both hands onto the counter in front of him so his physique is on full display. I like him—and not just the way he looks. He's sweet, respectful, and he's going to be a good time later tonight. His lighthearted banter will help keep all of us at ease in new territory, too.

"I thought I'd keep things fancy this evening, considering," I say suggestively.

"I like a lady that can ride that line," he says with a twinkle in his eye. "Cocktail, Coors Light straight from the bottle. Up for anything. You remind me of the girls back home." He starts working the bottles in front of him with ease as I grin at his compliment.

"Have you ever—" I raise my eyebrows at him and look around. I don't want to openly discuss the three-way we'll be having later, but I'm curious.

"Once or twice," he says with a cool smile as he twists another bottle open and hands a glass of white wine to a tall woman who's waiting to be served. I notice her watching him appreciatively when he grins at her.

God, he's sexy.

"How about you?" he asks.

"Never," I say with a smile.

"First time for everything," he says confidently. "I'll help you through it." My stomach spirals at the thought. I'm glad he's not bothered that I've never done this before.

"By the way, I introduced myself to the mate that'll be joining us," he says, swiping a towel across a drop of tequila sitting on the counter. "Didn't want our first meeting to happen between the sheets, aye."

"Oh, you did?" I cringe a little picturing Aaron shaking hands with Channing as they sized each other up and imagined a night with me in the middle.

"Yeah, he seemed a little hesitant about the whole thing, to be honest," Aaron says lightly, brows furrowed. "He's cool with me being there?"

"I think so," I say, praying Channing isn't getting cold feet. We've come this far.

But he interrupts my thoughts.

"Okay, but if he doesn't show—" He licks his lips as he trails off, raising his brows. He wants to know if we'll still be having sex, even if Channing backs out.

"Let's just hope he shows," I say laughing, then I reach over the counter and squeeze his shoulder before leaning in and asking, "I should probably know your last name. What is it?"

"Birrani," he answers over the music, and I nearly fall off my stool.

"I'm sorry, did you say Birrani?" I can't stop my eyes from bulging out of my head. "As in, Aaron Birrani?"

Aaron holds up a finger to his lips with a smile and looks around. His light green eyes sparkle at me playfully.

"You're really Aaron Birrani?" I confirm, because I cannot believe this. "What the hell are you doing behind the bar?"

"Mixing with my customers," he says nonchalantly with a tantalizing grin.

I'm speechless. And I am not hiding it well. Aaron Birrani is the sole heir to the Birrani empire, the biggest distillery and distributor in the world. His net worth back in Australia has to be in the multibillion-dollar range. I've come across his name countless times in my database. But this still doesn't explain why a man like him would be playing mixologist aboard the *MaryLou* this week, so I look at him expectantly for a better explanation.

"I told Owen I would celebrate with him this week, but I wanted to spend some time behind the bar, mixing with the people who enjoy my line of drinks. It's where I got my start when I worked under my father years ago, and I've kind of missed it."

I watch him light up as he tries to explain it all. He waves his hands toward the deck of partygoers around us, then motions more intimately between us as he continues. "This. I miss the part where I get to forget about spreadsheets and reports to just hang out with the partygoers behind the bar. This is fun for me. And I figured no one would recognize me in this crowd like they do back at home on the Gold Coast, so Owen agreed I could spend some time back here serving guests. To be honest, it's been kind of the highlight of my week."

I study him with a new appreciation, making a mental note to ask Daisy to update his notes and background information in our database. This man needs to be matched with one of my clients *ASAP*.

"Makes sense. It's nice to be a face in the crowd once in a while," I say, my lips curling into a smile. He's wildly success-ful, gorgeous, and humble. "Well, I'm very pleased to officially meet you, Mr. Birrani." I hold my hand out to shake his like we're meeting for the first time. He turns it over and kisses the top instead.

"It's just Aaron." He smiles, letting our hands linger where they're touching.

"And you're still on for … tonight?" I ask, finding it un-believable that I've reeled in Aaron Birrani as my third wheel.

"Nothing has changed," he replies warmly. "Just don't spread the word about this, uh, bartender thing out here, aye?"

The woman to my right, a young actress I recognize, or-ders a martini before adding, "And make it extra dirty, please." Then she turns to nudge me. "My god, he's *gorgeous*," she stage-whispers loudly before turning back to Aaron—obviously hoping he's overheard her.

He nods at the actress, then winks at me, smiling.

I laugh and grab my French 95 off the bartop, reeling over the fact that I'm going to be ravaged by both Channing Stanbury and Aaron Birrani at the same time before the night is through.

32

I spend the next couple of hours on the dance floor with Owen and our group of friends—including Cadence, who seems to warm back up to me as Owen showers her with more attention. We're all dancing and singing at the top of our lungs. It's a mix of old classics and current hits, each song beloved and belted out by everyone on the deck.

A curated group of superstars is taking turns completing their music sets, some of them debuting remixed duets of their top hits before delivering a personal toast to Owen. Since investing the money from his first company's sale, he's had his hand in almost every type of business over the years—from real estate to music labels and recording studios, so many of these artists know him well. And it's clear they love him like I do.

With each toast, Owen smiles from ear-to-ear, lowering his head and flushing slightly. The crowd on deck is loving it. Me, most of all. Seeing Owen cherished by this eclectic, powerful mix of friends just might be the highlight of the whole trip for me. At least so far.

If Channing has made it onto the deck tonight, I haven't seen him yet. But he'd better grace my stateroom later so I can tell Audra that his audition is officially complete, and he's ready to be matched with her. I look around as happy, singing faces bob up and down to the beat all around me. I don't want to leave, but at least I'm excited about where I'll be going.

I grab Owen's wrist and turn it over, lifting his vintage Rolex up to my face and squinting at the tiny clock hands.

Four minutes until ten o'clock.

Owen's eyes meet mine. He's fully aware of what I have scheduled for tonight. I shoot him a sorry sort of smile, and the light drains from his face before he can quickly recompose himself.

"Time to go?" he says next to my ear so I can hear him over the music.

I nod my head against him.

"Okay," he murmurs. He gives me a hug that lifts my feet off the ground, but the dancers around us barely notice. He gently lowers me back down to the ground and presses a kiss into my forehead.

"I love you, babe," I say into his ear. "Happy Birthday." He squeezes me even tighter before letting me go.

Then I turn and disappear into the crowd, pushing my way toward my stateroom.

It's go-time.

3 3

The door to my stateroom is already open when I arrive.

When I walk inside, my eyes land on Aaron. He's standing by the fireplace, the lights dimmed all around us.

"Hey there, love," he says as I enter the room and lock the door behind me. I am not making that mistake again.

"I used the key you sent me. Hope that's all right."

"Of course," I say happily, glad he's already here. But where's Channing?

I give him a quick kiss on the cheek. Then he hands me a freshly made French 95 that he must have brought with him from the bar. It's just as beautiful as the one he made earlier. "I thought you could probably use another one of these."

"You read my mind. Thank you." I take a sip, letting the orange-blossom scent fill my lungs "Have you seen—"

"I'm right here," Channing says deeply, walking in from the balcony doors. I breathe a sigh of relief. He's here.

Channing strides across the room and gives me a lingering kiss on the lips, then a tight hug. I squeeze him back. A song floats into the room from the open balcony doors and I can hear the party raging on the deck below. A wild piano solo takes over while the artist starts talking about the first time he met Owen. It's another birthday tribute.

I hit the button on the keypad to close the balcony doors behind Channing to drown it out. That's not exactly the background noise I'm looking for right now.

I hit another couple of buttons, and soft mood music starts playing through the room's central speakers. *Much better.*

Channing takes a swig of scotch from the tumbler in his hand. He nods at Aaron, and the two men smile. They're not exactly chatting it up, but that's okay. We're not really here to talk.

Channing hands me the glass. Just like our first night together. I smile at him warmly and take a sip from where his lips just touched the glass, still holding the other drink Aaron made me. It occurs to me that Aaron might be the least nervous one in the room. Though of all of us, he has nothing to lose.

I hand the glass back to Channing.

"Tonight is all about whether I can share?" Channing asks quietly, eyeing me then Aaron.

"It is," I answer. He swirls the glass, watching the amber liquid slosh around in a line before letting his eyes lock with mine. I shift on my feet, not knowing where he's going with this.

"All right then. Aaron," he says, turning away from me, "come kiss her."

I look at Channing in surprise.

"What?" I say, nearly laughing.

"I'm sharing," he adds seriously. Light from the fireplace dances across his features, making his smile look a bit dangerous.

Aaron wastes no time walking up to me. Without hesitating, he grabs me by the waist and pulls me in. His kiss is electric. Firm, smooth, and passionate right from the start. I hold onto his thick forearms to steady myself as he pulls me harder against him. When he finally lets me go, I look over at Channing breathlessly. He's watching us intently.

"Again," he says.

Aaron pulls me to him again, and I melt against his body as he runs his hands down my neck. Our hips push squarely against each other, and I can already feel his body starting to respond to mine. His hands caress my back and push through my hair, sending a shiver tingling down my spine. Then his tongue pushes into my mouth with just the right speed and precision, and I let him explore my mouth as his urgency grows stronger. When he leaves me breathless a second time, I grip his hips tightly as he starts kissing down my neck. Tiny shockwaves course down my body each time his lips linger on my skin.

I open my eyes just a crack to peek at Channing. He's standing by the fire, watching us. He takes another sip of scotch and licks his lips afterward. This moment—him watching me as Aaron drags his tongue across my collarbone—is sexy as hell. It feels incredibly intimate—erotic even—as our eyes meet with another man between us.

I hold eye contact with him while I wrap my arms tighter around Aaron and let my head fall back, finally closing my eyes to enjoy the feel of his lips against my skin.

When I lift my head, I see that Channing's eyes are still glued to me while Aaron starts kissing me on the mouth again. I get lost in his kiss, and close my eyes again to focus on him. But behind my eyelids, I can still picture Channing's gaze on both of us.

I slide my hands down the front of Aaron's body, and his abs feel like a washboard hidden underneath his shirt. When I get to the taut skin of his waistline, I kiss him on the mouth and glide my fingertips along the material between his navel and pants zipper, sweeping my fingertips back and forth along his hips. He pulls me into him again. I grab onto his biceps to stay upright. The size of his erection against me has grown even more impressive, and I look at Channing to see his face while I feel it.

"Take off your dress," Channing says and I glance over at him coyly in return. "Please," he adds, which makes me smile. He throws me a wink that tells me he's enjoying himself.

"I've got it," Aaron says. He turns me around and steps behind me so I'm facing Channing now. Channing is just a few feet in front of me and I watch his face as Aaron slowly lowers my dress zipper. One slow inch at a time. He's trailing kisses down each vertebrae as my skin is exposed to him.

Goosebumps spring onto my skin and my nipples harden as Channing continues to watch me from the front.

When Aaron gets to the bottom of my dress zipper, he reaches toward my hemline to tug it down, but I stop him.

"No, let me," I say, grinning at both men. I slowly slide each strap off my shoulders, then let my dress fall to the floor in a puddle around my feet so I'm standing in just my ivory bodysuit and heels. Aaron immediately grabs my waist from behind and kisses the back of my neck. I gaze over my shoulder to give him another smile.

"Damn, Cher," he breathes out. "Remind me to thank you later for the invitation to join you guys tonight."

"Why not thank me now?"

When I glance at Channing, he's already closing the gap between us. He reaches for me then lifts me by the hips. I let out a laugh as he tosses me down across the bed behind us. "Time to play," he says huskily.

My view is unreal. I lean back on my elbows to take both men in. They pull their shirts up over their heads at the same time. Deep tans, rippling muscles in the firelight, and practically fighting over me as they climb on the bed on either side of me on all-fours.

Aaron's tattoos across his bulging muscles make him look like the more rugged of the two, but Channing's face is more serious and focused than Aaron's as he climbs higher on the bed and starts kissing me deeply on the mouth. He's every bit as passionate as he was during the storm.

With Channing still kissing me, Aaron brings his hand up my legs, caressing the curve of my hip and up across my stomach. He draws a tight circle around my hip bones, up around my navel, and back down again as he watches Channing kiss me.

Channing tugs at the top of the bodysuit to free my shoulders, then my breasts, while Aaron trails light kisses around the bones of my hips, down toward my inner thigh. Every inch of me perks to life as I'm showered in attention from two mouths, four hands, endless sensual touches. Aaron pauses long enough for Channing to pull my lingerie all the way off, and I lay naked between them as their eyes drink me in from head to toe.

Channing suddenly pulls away from me as Aaron starts to kiss down toward the soft mound between my legs. Then Channing slides himself to one side of me before leaving one long kiss gingerly between my legs. I shudder lightly. The view of both of these men below my waistline nearly has me panting.

"I want to watch this first," Channing says. My whole body fills with warmth as my heart pounds.

Aaron responds by pushing my knees apart. I watch Channing's face as Aaron takes me in his mouth. Channing's eyes meet mine briefly, before he looks at Aaron between my legs. My entire body is absolutely on fire.

Before long, Channing is at my breasts, working my nipples between his firm hands and mouth, stealing glances toward Aaron playing hungrily between my legs. I'm left almost teetering over the edge as I watch both men work to destroy my inhibitions while my legs go weak. Then Channing stretches up to cup his hand over me, right under Aaron's mouth, and kisses me on the mouth once more before I get the chance to scream out in pleasure.

"My turn," Channing says. It's an order, not a question.

Aaron moves over and starts kissing my neck, while Channing grabs my hips and pulls me down hard toward his mouth, picking up where Aaron left off.

When his lips make contact, I arch my back and push into him, then relent into the sheets again. I want to make this last. I reach down and grab Aaron's erection in one hand, and push my other hand against Channing's hair. If he keeps this up, I'm going to explode.

"Don't stop," I manage to gasp. He picks up the pace, working me with his tongue, while Aaron begins rolling my nipples between his lips and tongue. I have to have one of them inside me. *Now.* "Please, give it to me," I moan.

"You," Channing says, barely breaking stride with his mouth while Aaron puts on a condom.

Channing watches us as Aaron pushes his cock into me, sliding in and out. His eyes flick from my eyes to between my legs. It's unbelievably hot. I have to have him inside me next.

Aaron is a machine, pumping in and out so fast, I can barely make myself hang on. I need to give Channing a chance. I hold my breath as Aaron comes hard, a moan escaping him just as Channing pushes his way inside me. Channing leans his head against me, gently biting the spot where my shoulder meets my neck. The pleasure is so intense I can barely hang on while Aaron watches us intently.

Channing makes it just four thrusts before I finally allow myself to give in, nearly screaming out as I ride the waves of ecstasy while he finally comes too.

I roll to my side, gasping for air and dizzy with pleasure as I take in what has just happened.

The room comes back into focus and I can hear the soft music whispering in through the speakers again.

"Best invitation I've ever had," Aaron murmurs into a pillow next to him, and we all laugh out loud together.

* * *

Once the three of us recover, Aaron heads back to his room. That leaves just me and Channing to bask in the post-sex glow by the light of the fire.

We lay breathless in the dark, curled up next to each other in the firelight.

I roll into him and allow myself to do something I haven't done since I was engaged, back before my heart split into a million pieces. I rest my head on his bare shoulder and hug my naked body against his, then he carefully wraps his arm around me and I push the full length of my body against his, reveling in the feeling of his skin pressed up against mine.

Channing has no idea how intimate this part is to me. The part where we just lay here, feeling each other's heart beat as we simply allow ourselves to be felt, and to feel. For me, this is more intimate than sex. As much as I love the rush, the pleasure, the fun, this right here is what I'd call *making love.* Lying together in the dark, tangled up with the feeling of happiness and satisfaction hanging in the air between us. This is the part I've missed the most for the last ten years.

And it feels good. So, so good.

I close my eyes—committing this moment to memory. The sound of my heart beating next to his. The scent of his skin masking the faint salty air that clings to him out here on the sea. Firelight dancing across his perfectly taut skin, and the taste of his lips still lingering on my tongue. I memorize the feeling of Channing's body, and his skin wrapped up next to me—and how it all worked together to make me feel safe tonight. Loved, even.

Tomorrow, I'll give him to Audra, but I don't feel torn about it anymore. I might be giving him away, but my heart is full of gratitude for the gift he's given me. For feeling whole again. And capable of love. I'll always have that.

Then I slip into a deep, peaceful sleep with a smile on my face.

3 4

I wake up the next morning to Channing's hand gently rubbing up and down my spine in long, slow strokes.

I roll over and open my eyes sleepily.

"You're beautiful in the morning," he says, looking down at me. I close my eyes and smile wider. The scent of fresh coffee hits my nose and my eyes pop open. "How do you drink your coffee, by the way?" he asks.

"You read my mind," I say as I sit up, giddy that a man is bringing me coffee in bed for the first time. We fell asleep intertwined in bed last night. I haven't done that in a very, very long time. Everything about it was perfect. "Usually I'll go for a macchiato, but I take my coffee right out of the pot when I'm this tired. Black and pure as night."

"You savage," he says, grinning. He gets up off the bed to pour two steaming mugs before climbing under the covers with me again. The curtain is already open so we can watch the sun sparkling off the waves outside. I realize how happy I am to see it.

"I wasn't sure I could go through with it last night," Channing says after he takes a sip.

I nod. My hunch about him getting cold feet was right. "You're not as much of a playboy as the tabloids have made you out to be, then?" I nudge him playfully.

"What do you mean?"

"I just got the impression … that you'd done that sort of thing before," I say more seriously.

"Oh, I'll do that kind of thing all day long," he says. "But it's different when the girl in the middle …"

He trails off. "When the girl in the middle is …?" I prompt him to finish the thought.

"Multiple partners can be fun, obviously. Last night was, well, you were incredible. But I couldn't stop thinking I'd rather have you all to myself." He eyes me, like he's afraid of what I might think.

My chest flutters a bit. The only reason I went through with this audition is Audra. Is he saying what I think he's saying?

I decide to keep it light. My feelings for Channing run deep. Maybe too deep. But I've already mentally handed him over to Audra. "It was a lot of fun," I say, "but I'm sure Audra will want you all to herself most of the—"

He shakes his head, like I'm not understanding. "It was fun. But I didn't agree to last night for Audra."

I raise my eyebrows, my heart beating fast as I brace myself to hear what he's about to tell me next. *Don't say it.* I beg him. *Don't. Just let last night be beautiful and fun. Then let me hand you over to Audra.*

"You know I have feelings for you, Cher."

My heart constricts. *He's going there.*

He continues. "I thought you had feelings for me too. That maybe last night would change your mind. If … if I showed you that *I* could share. Not for Audra, but for you."

He trails off and sighs, averting his eyes. He shifts in the bed, and I can tell he's feeling uncomfortable the longer the silence stretches between us.

"What we had last night was … it was magic. So was the first night we spent together. But I owe it to Audra—"

"Forget Audra," he says, looking at me pleadingly.

My heart sinks. Whatever happens next, I know I can't match him with her. He's not ready for that. He won't be the man she needs.

"I know you feel something for me," Channing insists, finally meeting my eyes. "I know we just met, but it feels like I've known you for so much longer. I could give you everything—love, a life without all this. You wouldn't have to do this job anymore, and—" He stops abruptly when he sees hurt fill my eyes.

Wouldn't have to do this job. He thinks I'm doing this because I have to. Which means there's a big part of me he doesn't understand at all.

I swallow painfully. "I love my job," I say finally. He's right. The feelings I have for him are brimming right beneath the surface, but this could never work. Not just because of Audra, but because of what he just said. He can share me for a night, but he'd never be okay with me continuing to run Match 360.

I wait for him to reply, but instead, silence cuts through me like a knife. I turn to face him more clearly. "This is how my business works," I say slowly, letting that thought settle in before continuing. "I've worked so hard to build it into what it is. I find people love. Mind, soul, and *body*. Other than the fact that there was an extra man in the bed last night, it was a pretty typical evening for me."

He shakes his head, pleading with me to let it all go.

"I love the life and company I've built," I say, the truth of it welling up inside me. "I'm proud of it. I genuinely make a difference in a lot of people's lives. There are families and babies and real love stories existing in the world that would have otherwise never been—all because of what I do." I pause, hoping some of this is getting through to him. "You might not understand it, but I truly, deeply love what I do," I say calmly.

"So you're going to choose meaningless sex over love?" he asks quietly.

I shake my head firmly.

"Why do I have to choose?" I'm not willing to give up everything I have for someone who won't take me as I am. "When I'm auditioning someone, there is no *making love*. It's just sex. Fun, sure. But just sex." I take a deep breath. "You're the first person I've made love to in ten years, and that means more than you'll ever know."

He considers this quietly for a moment. I can see the wheels turning in his head as he stares down at the floor, rubbing his thumbs across the back of my hands mindlessly as he takes in what I'm saying.

He sets his jaw, and I fight to keep sudden tears from spilling out. I love my life, and I love what I do. He's offering me his heart—but at the expense of everything I've built for myself. It's everything that I am.

"We're not a match," I finally whisper. "Loving me means wanting all of me. The good. The raw. And the unconventional."

I can barely breathe as I wait for him to speak next.

"I don't want to lose you," he says gruffly, but he's not looking me in the eye when he says it.

He sets his mug down on the nightstand before taking mine from my hands to set it down next to his.

He takes my face in his hands to kiss both my cheeks, and then my forehead. He brushes my hair off my face, and stares deeply into my eyes again before drawing my mouth to his. At first, his kiss is passionate and fierce. Then slow and sweet, until he pulls back to search my eyes.

I already know it's a goodbye kiss.

3 5

Owen and I are sitting at the longest dining table on the top deck.

Just a few hours ago, Channing left my room to get his things in order to leave the ship. I'm still in shock after what happened, and I haven't had the heart to call Audra yet.

I still can't believe everything that's happened this week.

Owen is seated at the head of the table, and I'm to his left with a substantial breakfast buffet laid out before us. The crew is giving us a sendoff fit for a king. Guests have been joining us on deck to gather plates of food throughout the morning and to wish Owen one last happy birthday before departing the ship. Choppers and boats have been ferrying guests to the private airports on shore all morning, and the *MaryLou* is almost empty now.

Cadence came by earlier, before she took off in the chopper with Charlie Beckett. She and Owen spent last night together. And from the way she was looking at him this morning—with hearts in her eyes—I'd gamble that she's hoping it means she and Owen are in a serious relationship now. She curled into him like a kitten when they embraced, then shared a lingering kiss while I tried not to watch.

I'm happy for Owen, but I can't help the twinge of longing when I think of him and Cadence sharing their bed and bodies together. Owen deserves to be happy, but the idea of sharing him—even platonically—with Cadence is going to change things between us.

It's pretty clear she hasn't truly warmed up to me yet as Owen's BFF who also just so happens to be female. She suspects I secretly love him. And the worst part is that she's sort of right.

Channing took off in his own unmarked chopper shortly after our conversation in my bed this morning. He was sweet enough to swing by the dining table to say a quick goodbye to Owen and give me a flustered kiss on the cheek before leaving us alone again. He said something about staying in touch, but I'm not sure how likely that is.

I hope I'm wrong. My heart aches a little when I think about what we shared—and the idea that I might never see him again. He wants me, but not all of me.

I can't do that. I've compartmentalized important parts of me for too long. And I'm not going to do that anymore.

After Channing left, I started to tell Owen what had happened with him last night, but another guest came over to wish him happy birthday before she departed. Then another. And another.

Now that we're finally alone, with the exception of the *MaryLou* crew busily preparing the ship to sail to a port large enough to dock the vessel, I'm gearing up to tell him the whole story. We'll be taking the last helicopter to shore, and then Owen's private jet will take us back to the States soon after.

My stomach rolls when I remember that I still have to break the news to Audra that Channing isn't her match. And, I'm bracing for my name to hit the tabloids hard when she shares the news with her friends. I put my forehead on the table and contemplate whether I should jump off the bow of the ship now or wait until after breakfast.

Owen puts a hand on my arm. "Hey, sunshine. Tell me what happened last night." When I look up, his kind, blue eyes are studying me intently.

"It's a long story." I sigh again, lifting my head off the table. I shed a few tears after Channing left my room this morning, but I have yet to let the floodgates really open and I'm not about to do that on the morning of our last day here. At least not until I am totally and completely alone with him on the plane in his private cabin.

"Try me," he challenges just as Kaylee approaches our table.

"Excuse me, Miss Thatcher. Just wanted to let you know that your belongings are packed. You're all set for the flight home." She smiles. "Is there anything else I can do for you right now?"

"I don't need anything," I say, turning to her. "Thank you so much. For everything." I've already left her a sizable tip on my bureau top, and I know Owen will be tipping the crew well for their impeccable service this week. Despite the storm and the attendees' unique needs this week, everyone seemed to have had a great time.

She smiles gratefully and hurries away.

I glance at Owen and scoot over so I can lay my head on his shoulder. "I know you like to throw wild parties, but this week was so much wilder than ever I could have imagined."

He laughs softly. "No kidding. And I'm pretty sure I haven't heard the half of it." He nudges my arm to signal that he's still waiting on the full story of last night.

I take a deep breath. "Where do I start?"

"Well, ten minutes ago, I watched you and Channing have the most awkward goodbye ever."

I laugh. This man does not miss a thing. As much as I sometimes wish that he would.

"What happened?" he prods.

"Last night was amazing. More than amazing. But …"

The whole story spills out of me. A play-by-play that ends with our conversation this morning.

When I'm finished, he's quiet.

"Wow."

"Wow is right." I laugh sadly. "Also, why didn't you tell me that Aaron the bartender is actually Aaron the distillery heir?"

"Oh, that." Owen looks thoughtful for a moment. "It seemed like he wanted to keep it on the down low so I didn't even think to mention it. He's a good guy though, right?"

I shoot him a playful glare in return. "Yes. That ba-zillion-aire turned out to be a great guy. Unlike Channing, he passed Audra's audition with flying colors …"

I freeze, as an idea suddenly occurs to me.

Aaron is exactly the type of person that Audra is looking for. She even mentioned she'd be very interested in exploring an adventure overseas.

I squeal with delight and tell Owen.

His face lights up in a slow smile. "I'm pretty sure he's still onboard." He nods toward the small group of people still milling around on deck.

I kiss Owen on the cheek. If Aaron is onboard, which I'm pretty sure he will be, we can finish the audition process in backward order. We'll share a few dinner dates back home to make sure he's going to be as good for Audra as I think he could be. And I've already verified his expert-level sharing skills in the bedroom.

I have a hunch he'll turn out to be a better match for her than Channing ever was.

36

Owen swirls the liquid in his glass around like a whirlpool, then drains it. He sets the glass down on the mahogany table affixed to the sleek leather chair that's more comfortable than any plane seat deserves to be.

Right before we left the ship, I managed to chat with Aaron—who was thrilled about the idea of being matched. When I told him about Audra, his eyes lit up. He's going to love her.

Now, Owen and I are watching out the window as the *MaryLou* becomes a tiny white dot against the brilliant blue sea in the distance. I'm leaning my head against his chest, listening to his heartbeat, letting everything that happened this past week wash over me.

To be honest, my heart still feels a little bruised. But I know now it's not broken past the point of working. Maybe it never was. I've just been keeping it locked away, afraid of what might happen if I opened it up to someone again.

I feel Owen shift toward me and draw in a deep breath.

"So, Channing finally cracked the code," he says quietly.

"Cracked what code?" I ask, confused.

He's quiet for a few more seconds. Then it comes out in a rush. "I've seen literally hundreds of men try to catch your interest over the last ten years. You've turned every single one of them down. You either match them with a client, or just flat-out reject them."

I listen, trying not to be jarred by this revelation. He's never said anything like this before.

He takes another deep breath before continuing, "I've been wondering … all these years … when you'd be ready to let someone in. I knew you weren't before. And that makes sense given everything you lost."

He pauses to let all his air out again.

Now it's my turn to raise my eyebrows at him, egging him on. *What are you saying, Owen?*

I don't know how to respond so I take a swig of champagne that the flight crew brought us before take-off, then shift my gaze out to the sea in the distance, below the plane.

I frown. "There's no *code* to crack," I say slowly, shaking my head. "You know how you just have that—something—a certain chemistry with someone?" I'm struggling to find the right words to describe how Channing made me feel. How I could fall for someone so quickly after closing myself off for a decade. None of it makes sense, but I can't deny how strongly I fell for him. And it certainly doesn't hurt that the feelings were most definitely reciprocated.

"Have you ever felt like someone just … fit into your heart like a puzzle piece?"

Instead of looking away, he rests his eyes on mine. He looks like he suddenly feels exhausted. "Of course I know what you mean," he says quietly.

I get the feeling he's talking about me.

Forcing myself to break my eyes away from him, I stare out at the water beneath us. But I bring myself back to look at him.

"Who?" I ask. I don't want to let it go this time.

He doesn't respond immediately. Instead, he breaks into a smile and shakes his head, looking down at his feet, then back at me.

My heart pounds as I brace myself for whatever he's about to say. I'm feeling raw and exposed after what just happened with Channing.

If he says it's Cadence, it will definitely hurt. But if he says my name, could I really take the leap? I think of the barely there kiss we shared earlier. It felt like flying. But flying comes with the risk of falling. What if we didn't work out? What if I lost him too? I feel that old pull to keep my heart safe—and sterile.

But I can't let it go.

"Who was it?" I bring myself to ask again. I let myself wonder what it would feel like to allow the feelings I have for him to fully blossom from the tight buds I've been forcing them into all these years. Was he waiting for me to let him know that I'm ready this whole time? Giving me the space I need? My head spins with questions waiting to be answered.

He stares at me, seriously at first and then he says quietly, "I think you know. I've felt that way about a woman for a very, very long time now."

I feel my cheeks flush.

We stare at each other for a moment.

Just as I open my mouth to let what's in my heart tumble out, the flight attendant bustles through the cabin door holding a bottle of fresh champagne.

"Thank you," we say in unison, watching the bubbly pour into our glasses gratefully.

She laughs as both of us throw them back like shots. "I'll be back with more?"

I nod, still unable to speak.

She pauses to say something about the weather in Malibu and the beautiful day ahead, but I can't focus on any of it. Instead, I stare out at the soft waves in the distance against a clear blue sky.

The storm is over, I remind myself. *You don't have to hide your heart anymore.*

The flight attendant is still talking to Owen, oblivious to the moment she's stepped into, when my phone vibrates. Unlike commercial liners, there's no need to turn off my phone. I look at the screen, fully intending to let it go to voicemail, when I see the name.

Audra.

For once, I smile with relief when her name appears on my screen. I tried to call her right before we boarded the plane, but she's calling me back now.

I glance at Owen. I desperately want to finish our conversation, but I'm also giddy to tell Audra the news about Aaron.

I've waited ten years to have this conversation with Owen.

I can wait a few minutes longer.

37

Audra's reaction is everything I hoped it would be.

"I need to hear every detail!" She practically shouts into the phone. "Aaron the ridiculously hot distillery king? Are you shitting me right now?!"

I can't help but laugh, both because I'm happy for her and because the knot in my stomach is finally able to unravel. Audra is happy. My business is going to be fine. This worked out so much better than the messy ending to everything that I had been dreading.

The flight attendant is walking away—finally—so I hurry to get off the call with her. Owen turns to look at me, and I feel a rush of love for that shaggy hair and tanned face.

"I promise I'll tell you more as soon as we land," I gush to Audra. "But I need to wrap something up right now. I'll call you as soon as we're back in the States!"

I hear her sigh, but I snap my phone off without moving my eyes from Owen's.

He breaks into a wide grin, and I don't even try to hide it as I take him in. I want to memorize everything about this moment flying over the world with him, but most of all, I want to remember *him*. My Owen. My irreplaceable Owen. Just like this.

Whatever he's about to say. Whatever happens next.

I want to remember this half-crooked smile playing across his lips, and those light turquoise eyes of his glittering at me. Like he always knows something I don't.

I glance at the endless, open water beneath us, and revel at how it doesn't make me feel scared anymore. I soak in the unmistakable realization that I'm finally going to be okay—and that maybe love does exist for me sometime soon in the future.

He leans toward me and gently kisses me on the forehead, then reaches for my hand and rests it against his knee. I silently add the feeling of his touch against my skin to the memory of this moment—another piece of our intricate puzzle that I don't ever want to forget.

I don't know what the future has in store for us. There's a million questions I want to ask about Cadence, about the last ten years. About what happened in college with that drunken kiss. But in this moment, all I know is that Owen and I belong together. Whether as two perfectly imperfect friends, or maybe as more than that. Because he's my person, my family.

And I know that I'm his.

"I just need to know one thing, Cher," he asks quietly. "Are you ready?"

NOTE FROM THE AUTHOR

If you enjoyed this book, a positive review would mean the world to me. Like other small-press authors, I rely heavily on word-of-mouth recommendations to reach new readers.

I can promise you that I read every single review. Because each one is a new window into this story. And because if you loved this book, *you're* the one I wrote it for—which is why I'm placing this note *before* the acknowledgments.

I'd love to keep in touch if you want to follow me on Instagram @brooklynbellauthor (you'll be the very first to know about new releases!)

* * *

One last thing: If you want to find out what happened between Cher and Owen (from Owen's perspective!) during that fateful college kiss, just scan this QR code! It'll take you to the free short story:

ACKNOWLEDGMENTS

Thank you to everyone who gave their time, talents, and support to this book.

Your insights, edits, and encouragement made this book so much stronger.

Thank you to my editor, Patti Geesey. I'm so grateful for your time and keen eye.

Last, but not least, thank you to my husband for being my final reader, my cheerleader, and best friend.

ABOUT THE AUTHOR

Brooklyn Bell began writing love stories for herself and her closest circle of friends when she was just twelve years old. She never stopped.

After completing a double major in psychology and creative writing, she continued living her best life through the sizzling heroines of her own romance novels while working in-house at an indie publishing press.

With five children, two naughty cats, and one great love story of her own, Brooklyn's writing serves as a great escape for both her and her readers. She is thrilled to bring you her debut series, *Matching Millions.*

Read on for an excerpt from book two in
the *Matching Millions* series: *More Than a Match*

1

My heart is pounding like a jackhammer in my chest.

Am I ready?

I can't find the words yet, so I just nod. *Yes, a million times yes.*

The expression in his eyes is like the sunrise after a storm: full of fire, full of hope.

I shift and lift the armrest on my own plush leather seat. The flight attendants are nowhere in sight. Part of me wants to take off my seatbelt and straddle Owen right here, without another word.

There's also a luxe private bedroom at the back of his jet that's a good option, too.

But there's a thought tickling the back of my mind. I've never vetted Owen—even though we've joked about it dozens of times.

What if I vetted him—for myself?

The thought sends happy butterflies spinning through me, and I smile as I lean forward to kiss him. It'll also help us figure out if we really are a good match without ruining our friendship by moving too fast, too soon.

His lips meet mine, warm and eager to explore. I kiss him back, letting the tip of my tongue twine with his for just a moment before grinning and leaning away a few inches.

"Let's not rush this audition process, Mr. Hawking," I purr.

He quirks an eyebrow. Then a devilish grin spreads across his face as he understands. This audition has begun.

Finally.

It's everything I can do not to take that handsome, familiar face in my hands and kiss him until we're both breathless. But I want to savor this moment, not rush it. Sometimes the foreplay is as delicious as the grand finale.

There's also the fact that, despite how exciting this moment is, I'm in solidly uncharted waters here.

I'm ready to give him my heart. I know that.

What scares me is all the potential surprises that might come up after that. The kinds of surprises I suss out for my clients with the vetting process. My matchmaking process works, and I want it to work with us.

He keeps his eyes locked on mine, waiting to see how this will go.

God, he's handsome.

God, I love him.

God, I want to fuck him.

The blush creeps into my cheeks. *Words first. Then body language.*

Thankfully, I know him so well already that the emotional and intellectual part of the vetting process won't take long. As

Saint-Tropez fades into the distance, I'm already debating whether we'll head to his place or mine the second this plane touches down in Malibu.

His place, I think with a smile.

"Tell me where we start, madame matchmaker," he says, his voice low and husky.

I think for a moment. I already know Owen like the back of my hand, so in a lot of ways he's as pre-vetted as they get. But I've never asked him the questions I've asked so many of my other potential matches.

I start where I often do when I'm dipping my toes into the water with a potential match: the fabulous Arthur Aron's thirty-six questions to fall in love with anyone. The famed psychologist created a list of questions that accelerate intimacy between two people in the shortest amount of time possible. I've found that to be true. Each question is a little more intimate than the last, and I pick and choose my way through them until I get a good read on somebody. Combined with body language, my own intuition and profiling skills I've developed over the years, and my assistant Daisy's recon on the backend, I can get a pretty accurate image of somebody very quickly.

Each question will give me a little more insight into what he wants out of a relationship, whether this will work, and what he's after. And who will make him happiest. I'll be watching Owen's face carefully while he answers. It's just the tip of our audition process, but by the end, I'll have a better idea of whether I can dive into his arms with zero reservations like I've wanted to do for so long.

I lean toward him and begin. "Let's start with a few questions. Answer however you want."

"Can I answer these from the bedroom?" He quirks an eyebrow again, keeping his eyes locked on mine.

I laugh. "Owen, focus!" He nods and kisses me one more time before I dive in.

I start at the top. "If you could have dinner with anyone in the world, who would it be?"

"You," he answers seriously, without hesitating even a beat.

I smile. I know he means it. I'm about to ask him my next question, when he says, "What about you?"

I tilt my head and study him. During all my years as a matchmaker, nobody has ever asked me the questions back. I'm about to tell him that it doesn't matter what I think—I'm the one digging around in his heart and mind. But then I stop. He's not just a potential match. He's my potential match. We should definitely play this back and forth. Will anything I say surprise him?

I'm about to find out.

I think for a minute. Then, because it's the truth, I say, "You'd be my pick for a dinner date, too."

He leans forward again, and my heart picks up its pace. He studies me and then says, "It's a date, then. Once we get back to Malibu."

My heart flip-flops. I can't believe this is happening.

2

Owen settles back against the soft leather of the cushioned seat that is so comfortable, it has no business being on a plane.

"If you could live until you're ninety years old and keep the mind or the body of a thirty-year-old for your entire life, which would you choose?" I ask, savoring every minute of this vetting process with him. His hand moves to my thigh, and a tingle of electricity moves through me.

"Mind," he says. "It's a gift to get old."

The way he says it brings a lump to my throat. If he'd asked me the question first, I probably would have said "body." My looks give me a lot of social real estate as a woman. But he's right. Getting old is a gift too many people I love didn't get.

"Same," I say softly, laying my head on his shoulder so he can't see that there are tears threatening in my eyes.

Each time I ask him a new question, he turns it back to me. And with each question, I fall deeper in love with him.

"Tell me the story of your life—in five minutes," I tell him, closing my eyes and shifting against him, so I can hear the sound of his heartbeat under my ear.

The beat of his heart stays steady while he thinks. Finally, he says, "I grew up in Holmby Hills, with my sister and my parents. My dad taught me to surf when I was ten, and it's one of the things I love him most for." He runs a hand lightly over my hair, smoothing it. "In high school, I was a goofy nerd on the inside, and a surfer bro on the outside. When I went to college, I sort of merged the two together. That's when I met you."

I smile, remembering the boy with the sun-kissed hair and smile I met at UCLA, back when I was studying fashion and psychology. I loved him from the start when the two of us got matched up to prep for a body language test in my Psych 101 class. While we were getting to know each other, he asked if I'd considered walking a line of wetsuits down the runway. I told him no, never, but it did give me the inspiration for my capstone project a few years later: an ocean-inspired line that featured clamshell gowns, billowing dresses that looked like anemone tendrils, and flowing dresses that looked like the waves rolling in.

I haven't let myself think about the outfits I meticulously designed and sewed for that show in years. Everything was so beautiful. I feel a surge of pride at how hard I worked, even if it did all fall apart.

Owen continues. "I studied Medical Engineering. My parents helped me get my tech company started during college. I realized pretty quickly that nanotechnology was the future of medicine, so that's the direction I went. I really wanted to make them proud. And ... I wanted to take care of you."

I feel a tear slip down my cheek against my will. I didn't realize that was part of the reason he worked so hard to build his business empire. I just thought it was Owen being Owen: smart, savvy, hardworking, and unbelievably talented. After what happened with my late fiancé Trevor and my family in the boating accident, I stopped going to classes. I never finished my capstone fashion line. Never took my psychology finals. Never got my diploma. But even more than that, I stopped getting out of bed. Stopped showering, answering calls, eating.

I was a mess.

Owen took me in. I knew he was hustling to make a name for himself in the cutthroat world of nanotech after graduation. I felt vaguely guilty for letting myself be persuaded to move into the second bedroom of his apartment. But I was so consumed with my own loss, my own heartache, that I never considered what that experience must have been like for him.

"I'm sorry," I whisper. "You took such good care of me then, but I know it must have been a lot. I'm so proud of you for everything you've built."

He shifts to look at me, tilting my chin toward him so he can see my eyes. I know they're rimmed in red. "You don't have anything to be sorry for. And I'm not finished with that story." He keeps his gaze locked on mine. "While I was building my empire, I got to spend every spare minute with my best friend. She went through a pretty rough time. The roughest. But we ate takeout together, and watched movies at night—she loves trashy TV and action films like *Mission Impossible* of all things. And I got a front-row seat to watch her take the shitstorm she'd been handed and bloom into the strongest, most confident, unique woman I've ever met. I've always been so proud of her. I hope we'll always be close. Until we're wrinkly ninety-year-olds with the minds of thirty-year-olds."

I laugh, but I can't hold back the tears anymore, no matter how much I try. I hate crying in front of anyone, Owen included, but keeping the emotion in my chest contained is like trying to hold back a waterfall with my bare hands. This all feels like it's been bubbling under the surface for so long between us. The release is overwhelming.

"Dammit, Owen." I laugh. "That was a really good answer."

"Your turn to answer," Owen says gently.

I draw in a breath. These were supposed to be the softball questions. But I'm already a puddle.

But I realize that I actually want to answer. I've never put it all into words before, and I suddenly know I need to. "I grew up in Rolling Hills with my sister, Ayla, and my parents. I had a really good childhood." I swallow and keep going. "We were always begging my parents to take us to Rodeo Drive, to look for movie stars." I laugh. "I think the only one we ever saw was the guy from Jeopardy. But we were still over the moon."

I nestle my head back against Owen's shoulder and wipe my eyes. "You know the next part of the story. I double-majored in fashion and psychology at UCLA. That's where I met you. And your roommate, Trevor."

I take a shaky breath. "After you graduated, I started dating Trevor. Things moved fast."

I leave out the part about how I kissed Owen the night before he left—then started dating Trevor the next day. At the time, I was reeling. I thought he'd rejected me. Trevor was there while Owen was away the year after he graduated, buried in his first acquisition that earned him over five-hundred-million dollars. And Trevor was wonderful.

I swallow and continue. "Everything was coming together with my capstone show. I was almost annoyed to have to take a break to go on vacation with Trevor to see my family at the end of that summer. There was just so much to do, with the wedding and the show coming up. And then … just like that, the boating accident happened, and everything turned upside down. I was alone. Except for you." I find his hand and squeeze it. "You saved me. Literally. You took me in, you gave me the idea for Match 360."

He squeezes my hand. "How many of our friends did you set up during college? It was practically a part-time job, even with your double major. Matching people was always second-nature to you. It just made sense to turn it into a career."

I smile and let out a long breath. "Thank you," I tell him softly. "For everything."

We talk for hours, hands entwined.

When the captain's voice finally crackles over the intercom, I jump in surprise.

Owen laughs and peers out the window.

The plane has already begun its descent into Malibu. The flight attendant hurries into the cabin to take our spent champagne glasses, putting a pause on our questions.

I'm about to suggest that we finish this vetting process at Owen's place—because I want to be near his enormous, comfortable bed when we do—when he glances at his phone as the plane wheels touch down.

"That's weird. I have three voicemails from my mom."
His brow furrows, and he looks up at me in concern as he holds
the phone to his ear.

I watch as his face shifts from concern to shock to panic.

"Owen?" I whisper, as my heart sinks.

He shakes his head numbly, and I know that whatever he's
just learned has just turned his world upside down—and mine.

www.ingramcontent.com/pod-product-compliance
Lightning Source LLC
Chambersburg PA
CBHW071459140726

47997CB00005B/1788